"You have a wife. You're married."

Zak dropped his arms, shoulders sagging, and on a long sigh said, "Yes. Technically, I guess I am."

Jilly wondered if God believed in technicalities, but figured now was not the time to ask. Zak was more than freaked out. She gripped his forearm with her fingers. He was trembling. Or was that her?

"I don't even know where she lives," he said numbly. "Or what she's been doing for the past ten years. But it's obvious she doesn't have much. She's broke and sick and alone."

Compassion, usually welcome, rose in Jilly. As much as she hated saying the words, she forced them out. "She needs your help. You have to give it."

"I know." Zak took her hand, a casual gesture, though he'd never done so before. He lifted her fingers one by one, traced a spray of freckles across the back, and then gripped her hand with such force, Jilly knew he was about to say something momentous....

Books by Linda Goodnight

Love Inspired

LINDA GOODNIGHT

Winner of a RITA® Award for excellence in inspirational fiction, Linda Goodnight has also won a Booksellers' Best Award, an ACFW Book of the Year Award and a Reviewers' Choice Award from *RT Book Reviews*. Linda has appeared on the Christian bestseller list and her romance novels have been translated into more than a dozen languages. Active in orphan ministry, this former nurse and teacher enjoys writing fiction that carries a message of hope and light in a sometimes dark world. She and her husband, Gene, live in Oklahoma. Readers can write to her at linda@lindagoodnight.com, or c/o Love Inspired Books, 233 Broadway, Suite 1001, New York, NY 10279.

The Last Bridge Home
Linda Goodnight

Love Inspired

Recycling programs
for this product may
not exist in your area.

™ LOVE INSPIRED BOOKS

ISBN-13: 978-0-373-87722-5

THE LAST BRIDGE HOME

Copyright © 2012 by Linda Goodnight

www.LoveInspiredBooks.com

Printed in U.S.A.

So do not throw away your confidence;
it will be richly rewarded. You need to persevere
so that when you have done the will of God,
you will receive what He has promised.
—*Hebrews* 10:35–36

For Diane in Dallas (You know who you are, girl!), who always reads the ending first and who can make me laugh with her warm, witty, encouraging emails.

Chapter One

A guy ought not to look that good in baggy old shorts and a holey T-shirt, but Zak Ashford did.

Jilly Fairmont yanked the rope on the cantankerous lawn mower and tried not to stare at her neighbor, cocked back in his lawn chair, shades in place, taking it easy on a sunny summer Saturday. She was surprised he wasn't playing baseball.

Yes, she noticed the comings and goings of her single neighbor. They were friends, buddies, pals. If she hollered, he'd come running. If he wanted someone to watch the game with, she'd be there in a flash. Zak didn't know it, would be shocked to even think it, but his best pal, Jilly, was in hopeless, unrequited love with him.

She yanked the rope again. No luck.

Across the quiet street and the rise of lush green lawn separating her home and his, Zak's voice called, "Hey, Jilly, need some help?"

No, she needed a new lawn mower. And a life. And she needed to stop mooning over her firefighter neighbor.

"I'm good. Thanks anyway." She backhanded the sweat from her eyes and yanked once again, muttering words like "trash heap" and "salvage yard" to the old mower. The incantation must have worked because the motor roared to life and shot black smoke and grass flecks from underneath.

With a wave toward Zak, she struck out across the thick, sweet-scented grass just as an unfamiliar car turned down her street.

Certain days in a man's life should come with warning labels. For Zak Ashford, that particular sunny day turned his world upside down, and nothing—not one single thing—was ever the same again.

He saw the battered old Chevy—a white Cavalier with a dented fender and one brown door—round the corner and rattle down the street in front of his house. Cars came and went. No big deal.

Kicked back in his lawn chair with a cold Pepsi at his side and fantasy baseball on his iPod, he focused on Jilly's dog of a lawn mower expecting it to wheeze and gasp to a stop at any moment. She'd need him over there pretty quick. Not that he minded. That's what friends were for.

He set his Pepsi aside ready to jog across the street to Jilly's just as the Cavalier chugged up the slight incline of his driveway, shuddered a couple of times and died. He pushed his sunglasses to the top of his head, leaned forward in the chair and squinted.

"Who—"

The driver's gaunt, pale face turned to stare at him. His belly went south. An electric current zipped from his brain to his nerve endings.

"No way. No possible way," he was muttering as he slowly rose for a better look. When he did, three small heads popped up from the backseat. Kids. A tiny blonde girl and two boys with dark hair. Not one of them had a child safety seat.

The adrenaline jacking through his blood centered on

that one thought. No matter who the driver, she was irresponsible. And she was breaking the law.

The brown door of the white Chevy groaned open before Zak reached it. A too-thin woman with short, curly hair—dirty blond—gripped the door and levered herself to a stand.

"Zak?" she said. "Zak Ashford?"

His belly did that dipping thing, like the time he'd fallen down a flight of stairs into the belly of the beast, a roaring fire. This could not be who he thought it was.

"Yeah, I'm Zak. Who's asking?" And why don't you have those kids in child restraints?

As he started around the car ready to give his fireman lecture, the woman met him at the headlights. "Remember me? Crystal?"

So it *was* her. She looked different—older, harder and more desperate, if there was such a thing—but here she was. His most humiliating moment.

Suddenly, the subject of car seats was not paramount.

Before he could open his mouth to ask why she'd come for this unexpected visit, she took two steps in his direction and crumpled like a wet paper sack.

With driveway concrete looming up fast, Zak's paramedic training kicked in. He lurched forward to stop her fall but missed. She collapsed against his bare knees and slid down to the top of his Converse All Star slip-ons. Gently, he eased to a squat and turned her over, going through the ABC protocol. Airway, breathing, circulation.

"Crystal. Crystal, can you hear me?" he asked, his hands and eyes assessing. Pale and gray, she looked like warmed-over death. A cloud passed between him and the sun. He shuddered, vaguely aware of car doors opening and people moving around him.

A small voice said, "Mama's dead."

The statement yanked Zak's attention from Crystal to a thin-faced boy. Maybe eight or ten, he stood solemnly, almost passively in front of Zak, staring down at his mother.

"No," Zak reassured. "She fainted. She'll be fine."

"Nu-uh," the boy insisted in that same tired, matter-of-fact voice. "She has cancer."

The word slammed into Zak's head as all the tumblers rolled into place. Crystal's ghastly gray color, her skeletal body, the ultrashort, curly hair all pointed to someone who'd spent recent time on chemo. Lots of chemo.

Another boy, this one a few years younger, started to howl. Weirdly, not one of the three kids standing in a semicircle touched the woman lying on the concrete. The third, a tiny blonde girl with wispy ponytails, stared with undisguised interest at Zak.

By now, Jilly had arrived, panting and breathless. "What happened?"

"She passed out."

"I saw that much." She leaned forward, hands on her knees to stare at his patient. "Should I call 9-1-1? Anything?"

"I am 9-1-1. Give me another second." He hitched a chin toward the kids. The yowler had escalated to something just short of siren velocity while the little girl had wandered off toward the street. "The kids."

"Oh, sure." Good old Jilly herded the toddler back to the fold. With one hand on the little one's arm, she hunkered beside the yowler and stroked his back. "It's okay. She'll be okay. Zak's a fireman. He'll take care of her."

The yowler wasn't impressed. The older boy was. His flat expression livened up a tad. "A real fireman?"

"Real deal," Jilly said. "He rides in a fire truck and everything."

Too concerned about his patient to bask in firefighter adoration from a grade-schooler, Zak checked Crystal's pulse again. Her eyelids fluttered. "She's coming around."

With a moan, Crystal opened her eyes and blinked blankly at her surroundings. She licked dry lips and managed a whisper. "What happened?"

"You passed out."

As she struggled to sit up, Zak offered his strength. At six feet three and one-eighty-five, he could have shot-put Crystal across the street. Careful lest he break her matchstick arms, he assisted her to her feet. She was light. Scary light.

"We should get you to the hospital."

She made a face. "Absolutely not. I've had my fill of those."

He turned her loose. She wobbled. He reached for her again. "Hey."

"I'm fine."

"Yeah, and I'm a unicorn."

She rubbed a shaky hand over her forehead. The three children, all corralled by Jilly, stared up at their mother. The yowler had stopped crying and was now sucking his thumb. The little girl had a very baggy diaper.

"Bella's wet," the oldest boy said, a hint of annoyed resignation in his voice as he headed toward the beat-up car. The passenger door opened with a groan and Mr. Serious dragged out a diaper bag, scraping it across the concrete as though it weighed a ton.

Zak's head buzzed on overload. What was Crystal doing here in his driveway after all these years? How had she found him? And why? She was sick, obviously, but what did that have to do with him? Now that she'd fainted in his front yard, what was he supposed to do with her? He couldn't stick her back under the steering wheel and send her out into traffic in this condition with a carload of kids. And no safety seats.

The older boy tugged on Crystal's hand while studying Zak with suspicious brown eyes. "Is this him, Mama?"

"Yes, Brandon. That's him."

Him what? Zak wondered, but his conscience kicked in. The woman, regardless of who she was, was sick and weak and shaking like one of Jilly's rat terriers at bath time.

"Come in the house for a minute," he offered. "I'll get you something to drink while you get your bearings."

He wasn't sure what else to do. Obviously, Crystal hadn't tracked him down to faint in his driveway and then go merrily on her way. But what she wanted remained a complete mystery—and from his experience, Crystal always wanted something. That's what had gotten him into trouble before.

With one hand on the wobbly woman's arm, Zak led the way into his house. His home was one of the modern few in Redemption, Oklahoma, a small historic town populated with big, beautiful turn-of-the-century Victorians and pretty little cottages. Today, he especially appreciated the lack of tall steps.

Once inside his spacious, slightly cluttered, ultra-male living room, the three children flocked around the mother like chicks around a hen.

"Mama, you want me to change Bella?" Mr. Serious asked, still toting the diaper bag.

"Yes, Brandon." Crystal took the little girl by the arm and pushed her toward Brandon. "Go over there in the corner, Bella. Brandon will change you."

Zak felt sorry for the boy, but it wasn't his place to interfere. "Can I get you some water or a Pepsi or something?"

She shook her head. "Nothing for me. The kids are probably starving."

Crystal was still Crystal. Needy and unembarrassed

to ask. "I've got baloney and wieners." What could she expect? He was a guy. Sandwiches and 'dogs were his mainstay. "Will they eat that?"

"Anything."

Jilly, who'd helped herd the children inside, spoke up. "I can make sandwiches, Zak."

Thank goodness for Jilly. He was a little rattled at the moment. "Thanks."

Jilly disappeared into his kitchen, knowing her way around from the many times they'd hung out. She was a pal like no other. And she made sandwiches and herded unfamiliar rug rats. Great neighbor.

"What's this little dude's name?" he asked, chin hitched toward the yowler with a thumb in his face. The boy looked a little old for thumb-sucking.

"This is Jake. He's almost seven. That's Brandon. He's nine. And Bella. She's three."

"Cute kids," he said politely although inside he was going loco. His heart thundered like a spring storm, his palms leaked sweat and every rational brain cell suspected an unpleasant reason for Crystal's visit. "So what's going on, Crystal? We haven't seen each other in what? Ten years?"

"About that." A ghost of a smile pulled at her gaunt cheeks, more of a grimace than joy. "I was really stupid back then, Zak."

Wary of apologies at this juncture, his anxiety jacked up another notch. "We were college kids. Stupid is normal."

She fidgeted; her skinny hands twisted in her lap. From the kitchen came the sound of Jilly digging in the fridge, cellophane crumpling—normal sounds—while in his living room sat the biggest mistake of his life.

"I shouldn't have gone with Tank that second time." Her

smile was wan. "Or the third. He was a jerk. Just like you said."

Tank Rogers had gotten her pregnant and dumped her—on Zak. Then, the creep had come back "for his woman."

"That was a long time ago, Crystal."

Her sigh was tired and whispery and full of regret. "I've made a lot of mistakes in my life. I don't want my kids to suffer for them."

Okay, what did that have to do with him? He sat with hands gripped together between his knees and waited her out, not knowing what else to do.

"I don't suppose you have a cigarette," she said.

"No."

She made a wry face. "I thought about quitting, but now I figure, what's the use? I'm sick, Zak." She drew in a shuddery breath. Hollow eyes focused on the boy in the corner changing his sister's diaper. "The doctors stopped treatment last week. I have cancer. I'm dying."

Even though he barely remembered this woman, other than the humiliation he'd received at her hands, the pitiful statement made him ache. He was a certified paramedic/firefighter, a serve-and-protect kind of guy, who liked people and wanted the best for them. Crystal was too young to die and leave behind three kids.

He shifted, cleared his throat. "I'm sorry." Sorry seemed a pathetically useless word in the face of death.

"That's why I looked you up, why I've driven across the state to find you. You have to help me."

Now they were getting down to the purpose of her visit, although he was still clueless. The sweat on the back of his neck said her reasons wouldn't be good. "You need money? I don't have a lot but maybe I can manage something."

She shook her head. Her gaunt body sagged against the fat pillow of his napping chair. "No."

"You sure you don't want to go to the E.R.?" Even a paramedic was limited in what he could do without equipment.

She brushed away the suggestion like a gnat. "No time, Zak. Please hear me out."

"Okay. Talk, but if you pass out again, you're going."

With effort, she gripped the chair arms and straightened. "Remember those days at college when you and I first got together?"

"Sure." How could he forget? She was pregnant with some other guy's baby, helpless and clingy, and he was an eighteen-year-old who thought he was the answer to her problems. She'd come to him, crying and needy, and he'd let her tears convince him to do something stupid.

Jilly reentered the living room, bearing a tall glass of orange juice, which she handed to Crystal. "You should drink something."

Zak noticed the grass stains on Jilly's shoes and the blades of grass stuck to the back of her shorts-clad legs. She'd raced to the rescue without a thought, leaving behind her uncut grass.

"Thanks," Crystal said wanly. She wrapped skinny fingers around the glass but didn't drink.

"I have sandwiches at the table if your kids are hungry." Jilly barely got the words out of her mouth when the trio launched themselves toward the dining room. Eyes wide, Jilly looked to Zak who shrugged. What did he know about Crystal's brood? Jilly hunched her shoulders and made a cute face. "I'll make sure they wash their hands," she said and hurried after them.

Crystal waited until the noise died down and Jilly's voice drifted between the rooms. Then she said, "You were the only person who ever treated me with respect."

What could he say except, "Thanks, I guess."

She smiled again, that odd stretching of cheeks too thin to handle the movement. "I should have stayed with you, Zak. I'm sorry for what I did. For the way I did it."

The unexpected visit was beginning to make sense. Crystal was seeking closure before she died. She wanted to make amends for her past mistakes, to the people she'd wronged. He couldn't help but wonder if there were others besides good old Zak Ashford on her list.

"If you came all this way to apologize," he said, "consider everything forgiven and forgotten. I have no bad feelings if that's what's worrying you." In fact, he never thought of her at all. Hadn't in years. "We did a dumb thing, but you took care of it and we both moved on."

Crystal set the untouched juice on his ottoman. Her hand shook. She grasped it with the other in her lap and squeezed, her fingers turning white as a hospital sheet. "That's what I've been trying to tell you, Zak. I didn't take care of it. Never did." She swallowed. "We're still married."

Chapter Two

Jilly lost her breath. She grabbed hold of the table edge to keep from crumbling the way Crystal had and strained to hear the voices coming from the living room.

Zak was married?

She put a hand over her mouth to keep from crying out. She was in love with a married man?

Oh, Lord, what have I done? Why hadn't Zak told her? They'd been fast friends since the day he'd moved in across the street and she'd loaned him a pipe wrench. How could he keep such a thing from her?

"Can I have more milk?" the smallest boy asked, holding up an empty glass.

With horror, she considered the three kids gathered around Zak's small, round table, cramming food into their mouths by the fistful. Were these Zak's children?

"Sure." The word came out in a croak. Numbly, she went to the fridge and poured more milk.

The blood that had drained from her head came roaring back to pound at her eardrums. She had to get out of here. She had no business listening in on this conversation, although she wanted every sickening detail. Common courtesy and the desire not to make a fool of herself kicked in.

She slapped a package of Zak's favorite cookies on the table. "You can each eat three. Okay?"

The oldest boy, Brandon, nodded. "I'll pass them out."

"Thanks." Not wanting Zak to know how upset she was, she took a minute to regain her composure, straightened her back and patted her hot cheeks. Then she walked as calmly as possible into the living room. The conversation ceased. "The kids are eating. I'll be at home if you need anything."

To his credit, Zak looked as he had the day he'd taken a line drive in the gut—stunned and speechless, like a fish out of water, his mouth open, searching for air. Clearly, he was not expecting Crystal to show up and reclaim their wedding vows. But she had. Without another word, because she wasn't sure she could say anything sensible, Jilly bolted out the door and raced home.

Mind in a muddle and heart pounding as hard as her sneakered feet, she blasted into the safe confines of the tidy frame house, the family home she shared with her mother. Two rat terriers met her, going airborne with excitement as though they hadn't seen her in a week. She caught Mugsy in mid-jump as he bounded to her knee and then catapulted against her chest. Satchmo, older and less excitable, plopped at her feet and looked up in adoration. Behind the wiry duo of terriers came her mother.

"What in the world is wrong? Did you get stung? Let me get the spray and I'll show those wasps a thing or two." Diane Fairmont waged an ongoing battle with a horde of red wasps that had taken residence years ago inside the eaves of her home. At fifty-six with ash-blond hair, much darker roots and too many cheesecakes on her hips, Diane also battled diabetes and high blood pressure. Jilly did not want her mother getting in a tizzy for any reason, certainly not red wasps.

"No, Mom. No wasps. I'm fine. Just…" She clapped her

mouth shut, not wanting to discuss Zak's personal life. She already took enough guff from her mom and two younger sisters about her friendship with the handsome fireman across the street. They would have a field day with this information. Living at home with her mother had its good points but the overinterest in Jilly's love life was not one of them.

"Then what is it?" Mom insisted. "You're white as a ghost."

Which meant every freckle on her face stood at rust-colored attention. Had Zak noticed?

"Maybe I got too hot."

"I thought you went over to Zak's." Mom went to the window and pulled back the curtain to gaze out. "Didn't I see a woman and some kids in his yard?"

Great. Mom had seen Crystal. Zak's *wife*. Jilly's insides started to shake. A wave of nausea pushed at the back of her throat. *Zak had a wife.* "I need some water."

Hurrying past her frowning mother, Jilly ran a glass of tap water and kept right on going through the laundry room and out the back door. She needed time to think about the stunning revelation. Time to peel the pieces of her shattered heart off the sides of her chest cavity.

Mugsy and Satchmo trotted along, eager for a run in the backyard. "Stay inside. Back."

The terriers skidded to a halt, dejected but obedient. Sorry to disappoint her two babies, she reached down and picked up the Frisbee from the back porch step and tossed it through the house. The two dogs zipped off after their favorite toy, happy again. She wished she could be that easily mollified.

Glad to be alone, Jilly walked to the left corner of the fenced backyard. Beneath a sprawling, thirty-foot maple, planted years ago by her now-deceased father, three pairs of pink eyes gazed out at her from a rabbit hutch. Fat, fluffy and friendly, all of them rescue rabbits dumped after Easter when they were no longer tiny and adorable, the trio awaited her attention.

People thought she was a soft touch, especially her sisters, but with a career as assistant to Dr. Trace Bowman, veterinarian, what did they expect? She loved animals.

She also loved Zak Ashford.

With a distressed moan, she opened the hutch, lifting each one to the grass. Then she plopped down beside them for a cuddle. Faith and Hop wiggled from her lap to explore. Lucky, the one-eared mini-lop who'd had a close encounter with a cat, remained where he was, snuggled safe in Jilly's arms. She pressed her face into his silky silver fur.

"He's married, Lucky," she whispered. "I don't know what to do."

Lucky, the good listener, sniffed the side of her face, whiskers tickling.

"Why didn't I know? Why didn't he tell me?" The shock had begun to wear off, but she still felt as if she'd swallowed a hot brick. She was in love with a married man. The bold fact of that statement went against everything she believed in. Wanting someone else's husband was a sin, a direct violation of the Ten Commandments.

And Lord help her, she didn't know how to stop.

Zak stared into the face of his past, stomach churning, sweat beading and wished he could run out the door and follow Jilly. He wanted to be anywhere but here with Crystal.

"You can't be serious," he said, incredulous. "You left me a note. You said you had filed for divorce."

"I meant to." She shrugged. "But you know how I am. I got busy and things happened…"

He recalled the helpless girl who couldn't remember to pay her electric bill, but a marriage dissolution was a tad more important. She'd wanted Tank Rogers, not Zak Ashford. That should have been enough to help her remember.

At the time, he'd been embarrassed by her betrayal, humiliated to have been duped by her pretty face and the way she'd wrapped him around her finger with her sob stories. He'd felt sorry for her. She'd been raised in the foster system, had no one to turn to, and Zak's ego was stroked by being her savior, the go-to guy who could make everything better. So much so that he'd followed her to the courthouse and married her to, as she'd put it, "give her baby a name."

The memory struck terror in him. "Your kids?" The chatter in the dining room made him lower his voice. "Whose—" He didn't know how to ask if his name was on their birth certificates. "Do you still use my name?"

"It's my name, too, Zak, so yeah, sometimes." Zak could hear the "when it's convenient" behind the words. That's the way Crystal had done everything. Whatever was easy and convenient. "But Brandon and Jake have Tank's last name—Rogers. He insisted."

Zak nodded, so relieved he thought he'd slither off the couch. "Good."

"Bella has yours."

An electric shock went through him. "What?"

She shrugged again and smiled, a glimmer of the charming-as-sin young woman she'd been coming through. "I had to put something."

"What about her father?"

"I don't know. I wasn't sure. He wasn't around. I wanted her to have someone good—"

Zak grabbed his head with both hands to keep it from exploding. "Whoa, Crystal, this is insane."

"I didn't think it mattered. You wouldn't know."

"You didn't think it mattered?" This woman was a nut job. And he was married to her!

"I wouldn't have come to you now if I hadn't been desperate."

He'd heard that before. The day she'd showed up at his apartment with bruises on her cheek crying that Tank had left her for good. He'd fallen for it then, but he was older and wiser now.

"Okay," he said, heart leaping around like one of Jilly's terriers. "Let's deal with this and get it over with. I'll pay for a divorce." He wrestled with that for a moment but won. As a man of faith, he didn't believe in divorce but this was different. Wasn't it? "An annulment would be better. We weren't married that long. What, a few weeks? A month?"

"Nearly ten years now."

"Stop it, Crystal. We're not married, never were. We had a piece of paper, and I gave you a place to stay and a sympathetic shoulder. We weren't in love. I filled a need until Tank wanted you back." He felt like a jerk for saying these things to her, but they'd been in the back of his head since the day he'd come in from class and found a note propped with a banana against his pillow.

"I never meant to hurt you, Zaky." The old, juvenile endearment grated on him. He'd fallen for it back when he was a boy, but he was a man now.

This was the way with Crystal. Charming and manipulative in an innocent way, she never *intended* any of the foolish things she did.

Zak studied her ravaged body, a shell of the vibrant, self-seeking kewpie doll that had crooked her finger and had him running. Zak searched his heart, his conscience, and prayed. Had he loved her? He'd been eighteen. He didn't know. He'd been in…well, not in love. Playing the knight in shining armor had made him feel like an adult, a man.

"Why are you telling me this now?"

"I told you. I'm dying."

That tiny niggling in the back of his brain started up again. Something buzzed around like a gnat, pestering, warning. "And you wanted to clear your conscience?"

"That's not why I'm here, Zak. I don't have time."

"What if I'd gotten married to someone else, Crystal? Do you realize what that would have made me?"

"No one would have ever known." She frowned, clueless. "I guess. I don't know. I didn't think about it."

She never had.

"Why didn't you contact me a long time ago? I would have dealt with this."

"Maybe it was fate."

Even for a guy who remained laid-back and calm when fighting a raging fire, he wasn't particularly surprised when sweat rolled down his back. "It wasn't fate, Crystal. There is no fate. There are only people making dumb decisions."

Crystal sagged back again, expression wounded. "I'm sorry. This is not going the way I'd hoped. I'm so tired. Sometimes I say things wrong."

Instantly contrite, Zak wanted to kick himself. She had cancer. She'd told him she was dying. What kind of jerk berated a dying woman?

Crystal's three children trailed in from his kitchen, munching on his Chips Ahoy! He looked at the little girl, dismayed and bewildered to know she bore his surname. His name was on her birth certificate. Was that even legal?

Crystal closed her eyes, a hand to her forehead. He hoped she didn't pass out again. But whether she did or not, he had a responsibility—not because they were still legally married, if that was even true, but because he wasn't the kind of man who could live with himself if he didn't offer aid to a dying soul.

"Let's start again," he heard himself saying. "Tell me what you need, Crystal. Is there some way I can help?"

Her eyes opened, still as blue as summer but without the spark of energy that had melted him years ago. She looked old and haggard. "That's why I'm here. I knew you'd help me."

"Help you what? I know a good doctor. Some nurses. I have some money put back. What do you need?"

"My kids." The three settled around her on the couch, painfully alert to the serious adult conversation. Weakly, she stretched an arm to each side like wings and covered them, a hen sheltering her chicks.

"When I die," she said, "I want you to take my kids."

Chapter Three

$\mathcal{Z}$ak wanted to say she was crazy. He wanted to yell, "No way!" He wanted to rewind to that blissfully ignorant time when he'd been admiring Jilly's jaunty lawn mower grit and Tim Lincecum's earned run average. If he could pitch like that he'd be in the majors.

Instead, he closed his eyes and tried to get himself under control while praying for a quick and easy resolution. None was forthcoming.

"This is sudden," Crystal said.

"Sudden" was a major understatement that left him gaping. Sudden was when the runner on first took off for second. Sudden was when he'd pitched a no-hitter and his teammates dumped the ice bucket over his head. This wasn't sudden. This was catastrophic.

"I wish I didn't have to spring it on you this way, but…" The remainder trailed away, lost in the facts. Crystal was running out of time. He wasn't cynical enough or cruel enough to question that part of her story. All he had to do was look at her ashen color, the black circles under her eyes and her emaciated body.

He tried to get a grip, tried to ignore the rampaging elephants in his chest and the shock ricocheting through his head to focus on the most important portion of this bizarre conversation. Crystal was dying. "The doctors can't do *any-thing?*"

"They've done a lot. More than two years' worth. Nothing worked. I waited too long." She lifted one very thin shoulder, puckering the dragon logo on her pink pullover. "I thought the lump would go away. Instead the cancer spread."

He could see her doing that. Crystal didn't want anything to be wrong, so she pretended it wasn't. This time, ignoring the problem would cost her everything.

"That's why you have to take my children. They're sweet kids, Zak. Not perfect, but you know what will happen if I don't find them a home."

"Foster care." He knew how much she'd hated growing up in the social system and how she'd wished for a family she'd never gotten. Now, she had one, in these children, and she was losing them. "What about Tank?"

She rolled her eyes. "I haven't seen Tank in a long time."

That figured, but still. "They're his boys."

"He's mean. He hit Brandon a lot." Probably Crystal, too, from what Zak recalled of Tank Rogers. "I left him after Jake came along. I've made a mess of my life but I love my kids. They deserve better."

The middle boy began to sniffle. The older one scowled and stared at the wall, a robot of a boy.

"Maybe the kids should go outside and play while we talk?" Zak suggested.

"Sure." Weakly, she pushed at Brandon. "Take Jake and Bella outside. Stay in the yard."

The stiff-backed boy trudged out, gripping his sister's hand. Jake trailed them, sucking his thumb.

When the back door snapped closed, Zak held out his palm as an olive branch. He intended to be kind but firm.

"I'll help you in some other way, Crystal, but I can't do this. I don't know anything about raising children, especially a little girl." The daddy word gave him cold chills. Maybe she'd see the folly of her suggestion if he laid out the facts about himself. "First of all, I'm single. They need a mother. And I'm gone a lot. My firefighter job comes with a crazy schedule. Plus, I play a lot of baseball."

"Still?"

What did she mean "still"?

"Dreams die hard." Hey, he was only twenty-seven. Roger Clemens won a Cy Young Award when he was forty-two. The majors could still come calling.

"The job, baseball, being single, none of that matters, Zak. My kids need you."

All those things mattered to him! "They need a caring family, Crystal. There are people out there who will adopt three cute kids. A family, not some single guy without a clue about raising them."

"Who? Name one person who would adopt three kids all at once."

"I don't know," he said, exasperated. "Someone."

If he told her to call child welfare, she'd go ballistic. He wouldn't do that anyway. But what could he do? He was not the daddy type.

"You're the only person I'd trust with them."

Oh, man. She was killing him. He wished like crazy Jilly was here to help him out. She'd know what to say. "Ask me for something else, but not this. I can't."

Crystal pressed shaky knuckles to her mouth but didn't cry. For that he was grateful. A crying woman was a powerful force.

On wobbly legs she rose, and with more dignity than he'd imagined she said, "I'm sorry to have bothered you. You aren't the man I remembered, after all."

* * *

Jilly heard car doors slam. She pushed off the grass, scratched at the itch on the back of her leg and carried Lucky to the corner of the house. From there she could see Zak's driveway. She rubbed Lucky's velvet ear and watched as Zak reached into his pocket, took out his wallet and offered Crystal some money. She must have refused because he leaned into the window to say something and tossed the bills inside.

The battered Chevy backed down the drive, children's faces pressed against the windows, and left Zak standing with arms dangling at his sides as they drove away.

Had there been some sort of ghastly mistake? Was she Zak's wife or not? If they were married, where was she going? And why was he tossing money into her car?

Hope sprang up like a tenacious weed. Maybe they weren't married. Maybe she'd misunderstood the conversation. After all, she'd been in the kitchen with three talking children. She'd made a mistake. Thank goodness.

Or maybe the woman was a nightmare from Zak's past and he'd paid her to go away. Maybe she'd come to extort money. Maybe…

Curiosity getting the better of her, she put Lucky and the other rabbits back in the hutch and went inside to wash her face and hands. She had to know. Yes, she was nosy, but Zak was her best friend. He needed her.

And she'd go crazy if she didn't know the truth.

Please let the conversation be a misunderstanding on my part. Zak could not be married.

"You look better." Her mother stood in the laundry room, folding towels into a green plastic basket. The smell of lavender fabric softener, moist and hot from the dryer filled the narrow space.

"I'm going over to Zak's. Don't get too hot back here. I can fold these later."

Mom, who worried less about her blood pressure than her daughter did, said, "I saw that woman leave. I wonder who she was. All those children."

"*You* had three children." Jilly snagged a clean washcloth.

"Mmm. Didn't seem that many back then." Mom kneed the drier shut with a metallic bang. "You don't think she's Zak's girlfriend, do you?"

Jilly's stomach lurched. She fisted the washcloth into a wad. "I wouldn't know."

"Did you watch that movie on cable last night? The one I told you about?"

"Yes, Mom." She'd watched the DVD a long time ago. The movie, about a girl who was always a bridesmaid and never a bride, could have been the story of Jillian's life. Except for the part about finding the guy of her dreams. Or rather *him* finding *her*. Jilly had found hers five years ago when Zak bought the house across the street. Beyond sharing pipe wrenches and hamburgers, he hadn't bothered to notice.

"That could happen to you if you'd stop jumping every time he calls." Mom handed her a stack of clean, fragrant towels. "Zak likes you. That woman is the first one I've ever seen over there other than his mother and you."

"Mom, let it go." Jilly hid her reddening face behind the stack of terry cloth. "Guys don't find me attractive in that way. Zak likes me for a friend."

"Maybe he'd like you for more if you played hard to get. Men are intrigued by a woman they can't have."

Jilly chanted her mantra, the one she'd used since she was sixteen. "When the time is right, the Lord will send someone."

Someone who didn't mind her freckles or red hair, someone who saw the real Jillian Fairmont. Not some jerk like
Clay Trent who'd called her "Spotty" in front of the entire
junior class. "Men don't find me attractive."

"You're too hung up about your looks, Jillian. You're a
beautiful woman."

Even though her mother repeated the words often, Jilly
didn't believe a word. Years of playground torment had told
her the truth. Boys weren't attracted to her. They wanted
to be her friend, her pal, but not her date to the prom.

"Bye, Mom."

"Take some of those muffins. The way to a man's
heart…"

Jilly made a rude noise but dumped the towels in the
linen cabinet and grabbed the muffins as she threaded her
way around a pair of squirmy dogs.

With Mugsy and Satchmo at heel, she jogged across the
street, her mother's words ringing in her head. She wanted
to believe Zak found her attractive, but he'd never treated
her as anything but a pal.

She hammered on his front door. "Hey, open up. I
brought Mom's muffins and two of your buddies."

The dogs alone usually brought Zak roaring to the door
to engage in a mock battle with the terriers.

"Come on in. I could use a friend."

Uh-oh.

Jilly gave the door a push and stepped in. Sprawled on
the couch, a dejected-looking Zak took a gut full of rat terrier as both dogs leaped aboard. He shoved them off. The
dogs plopped on their bottoms, heads tipped to the side in
a comical questioning expression. Clearly, their friend did
not want to play, an unusual turn of events.

"You don't look too happy." Jilly shoved his sneakered
feet aside and scooched in at the end of the couch. She set

the muffins on a lamp table out of the dogs' reach. "Who *was* that? What happened?"

Zak dropped his feet to the floor and sat up. "I need to talk to you about something. Promise you'll hear me out before you tell me how stupid I am."

She'd never seen him look this worried. The hope that she'd misunderstood dwindled away. "So, is it true? You're married?"

Shoulders bumping hers, Zak swiveled his long, lanky body in her direction. Green eyes stood out against a summer tan, bewildered. "You heard what she said?"

"If you mean Crystal, yes, most of it. At least, I think I did." Sickness rose in Jilly's throat. She fought it down, although every hope she'd ever had, every dream that Zak would wake up and see her as a woman instead of a pal died a quiet death. "Why didn't you tell me before? Why didn't I know?"

"Because *I* didn't know." He rubbed the back of his neck, kneading tight muscles. She'd done that for him before, after a hard ball game when his muscles ached and his arm stiffened up.

Before she knew he had a wife.

"Please," Jilly scoffed, even though nothing amused her. "Give me some credit here. She didn't give you one of those drugs that make you forget, did she? You married her. A man doesn't forget something that momentous."

"I knew I *had* married her. I just didn't know we *are* married." He slammed his fist onto his thigh. "This can't be happening."

"You're not making sense."

"Tell me about it. Nothing makes sense right now except I have a problem I don't know how to solve." He gripped the neck of his T-shirt and pulled, exposing the tanned skin below his throat. Jilly wanted to make him feel better, but how did a woman comfort another woman's husband?

Mugsy, the empathetic one, lifted both paws lightly to Zak's knee and cocked his head. Zak absently rubbed the pointed ears. Satchmo, not to be left out, leaped easily into Jilly's lap, dog tags jingling.

"From the top," Jilly said. "Explain this before I call your mother and tell her you're having a nervous breakdown."

"Whatever you do, don't call my parents."

"They don't know?" This was worse than she'd thought.

"Not everything. I was in college, away from home, on baseball scholarship. Crystal was one of those girls who hung around college guys even though she wasn't in school. Kind of a groupie type. She'd come to the ball games and jump up and down, all excited. After a good game, she'd rush up, gushing about how I was sure to get a call from the scouts."

"She stroked your ego."

"I guess. What did I know? I was barely eighteen and green as a frog." He made a huffing noise.

"So what happened?"

"You know that old song about the candle in the wind? That was Crystal, blowing through life at the mercy of anyone and everything. She had problems and I felt sorry for her." He shrugged, chagrined. "She was cute, too. Put the two together and I didn't stand a chance when she asked me to marry her for the sake of her baby."

"*Her* baby?" Even though the hated red blush crept up her neck, Jilly had to know. "Or yours, too?"

Zak's eyes darkened to the color of rich moss, eyes that usually made her heart flutter. She couldn't let that happen anymore. Even though it did.

"You have to believe me, Jilly. Those kids aren't mine. None of them. Crystal and I were married about fifte minutes. Shoot, most of the time I was at ball practice. I barely saw her."

The unbidden vision of Zak and Crystal together stirred in the pit of her stomach as powerful as a canine virus. She hoped she didn't throw up on Zak's tennis shoes. "How could your parents not know?"

"I was working my way up to sharing the news."

"They weren't going to be happy about it?"

"Not even close. I was on scholarship, shooting for the big leagues. My dream was theirs, too. They would have been crushed."

Jilly understood the feeling. She was crushed. Decimated. Shove a stick of dynamite in her heart and light the fuse.

"Her old boyfriend, the baby's father, came by one day while I was in class and away she went. Her note said she'd filed for divorce to be with her soul mate." He made a grim face. "Some soul mate."

Jilly straightened, a fragile glimmer of hope flaring. "Then you aren't married."

"I don't want to be. Never intended to be. At the time, I was too busy and dumb to consider she might not follow through."

Jilly's hope crashed and burned. "She didn't."

"No." Zak let out an agitated sound. Mugsy licked his hand in consolation. "Looking back, I should have known. Crystal wasn't the kind of girl who followed through with anything. Ever."

"Oh, Zak," she moaned. "You have a wife. You're married."

"No!" He slapped both hands to the sides of his head, fingers digging into his short brown hair. Surprised by the vehemence, the two dogs leaped to the floor. Zak dropped his arms, shoulders sagging, and on a long sigh said, "Yes. Technically, I guess I am."

Jilly wondered if God believed in technicalities, but figured now was not the time to ask. Zak was more than freaked out. She gripped his forearm with her fingers. He was trembling. Or was that her?

"Okay, let's think about this rationally," she said. *Yeah, right, and while we're at it, let's fly to Mars.* "Why is Crystal here now? What does she want? A divorce? Like in that movie, *Sweet Home Alabama?*" Please Lord, let that be it. If Crystal divorced him, Zak would be free. Then another, much worse thought hit her. "Or did she change her mind after all this time and want you back?"

Jilly hated the thoughts running through her head. Ways to get Zak out of a marriage when marriage was ordained by God. What was wrong with her?

She knew the answer to that one. She loved a married man. She wanted him for herself. What kind of horrible person was she?

"Crystal has cancer," he said flatly. "She doesn't have much time left."

"Oh, my goodness." Guilt rushed in. The woman was dying and all Jilly could think about was how to steal her husband. "She's so young."

She wanted to ask what Crystal's illness had to do with Zak, but guilt wouldn't let her. "Why did she come to you? For money? Or what?"

"I don't even know where she lives," he said numbly. "Or what she's been doing for the last ten years. It's obvious she doesn't have much. She's broke and sick and alone."

Compassion, usually welcome, rose in Jilly. As much as she disliked the words, she forced them out. "If she needs your help, you have to give it."

"I know, but I can't do what she asked. I just can't." He took her hand, a casual gesture.

"Tell me. Maybe I can help."

"I don't think so." He lifted her fingers one by one, traced a spray of freckles across the back and then gripped her hand with such force that she knew he was about to say something momentous. As if having a wife wasn't momentous enough. "She asked me to take her kids—" he hesitated "—after..."

Jilly frowned. What was momentous about that? Crystal was desperately ill with little time left. "Until her family comes for them?"

He released her hand and sat back. "There is no family, Jilly. No one. She doesn't have a single person anywhere to turn to. No one except me—the long-lost husband who didn't even know he was one."

Zak's meaning seeped in, slow and deadly as arsenic. He not only had a wife, but he was also about to become a father.

Zak watched the color drain from Jilly's face. Her freckles popped out like rust stars against a porcelain sky. She had beautiful skin, a fact he noticed every time she blushed, which was often. She made a tiny noise of distress and Zak resisted the urge to toss his arm over her shoulders and give her a hug. He didn't like seeing Jilly upset, especially when he was the cause.

"You sent her away," she said, blue eyes sad and dismayed.

"What else could I do? I'm not their father. I don't even know her."

"But now that she's gone, you're having second thoughts."

"Yes, of course I am!" What kind of man would he be if he didn't? He dragged both hands down his face and blew from his lips like a horse. "She's dying, Jilly. I feel like a piece of scum for refusing her anything. At the same time, I'm not the person for the job. I can't be a father to three strange, grieving, needy children. I don't want to be. I can't be. The whole idea is nuts." He was starting to get hysterical. Zak Cool, the pitcher with ice water in his veins and fire in his left arm, was teetering on the edge.

Jilly pushed Satchmo off her lap. "Go lay down."

"I wish I could," Zak said and when Jilly rolled blue eyes at him, he grinned a little at his joke. "Dogs are lucky. When something upsets them, they can go to sleep and forget about it."

Jilly wasn't amused. If anything, she'd gone even paler. A tiny, worried pulse beat in the hollow of her throat. "You're not a dog. You can't go to sleep and forget about it. So what *are* you going to do?"

"I don't know. I gave her some money. She was broke, exhausted, sick." He scrubbed his face with both hands, not that it did a bit of good. "Man, I'm a jerk."

Jilly pushed at Satchmo who tried to regain her lap. "Was she going back to her home?"

He hadn't asked. He'd been so busy getting her out of his house, his driveway, his life that he hadn't asked what she would do or where she would go. "She looked tired. I suggested she go to a motel."

"Kitty's place?"

"Yeah." He'd soothed himself with the thought that Kitty Carter ran a clean, safe, reasonably priced motel. "Maybe I should call Kitty and ask her to keep an eye on them."

"I don't know, Zak. This doesn't seem right to me."

"Nothing is right today. I want a replay."

"I'm sure Crystal does, too."

"Thanks for kicking me in the teeth," he said wryly. "I deserved that."

"Maybe you should go over there and bring them back here."

"Here? To my place? Are you nuts?"

"Regardless of the particulars, regardless of when or why you married her, she's legally still your wife."

"What if she's lying?" he asked, desperate to be free of this problem.

"Wouldn't that be easy to check?"

"I don't know. Maybe. Maybe she's only saying this because she remembers me as a soft touch."

"Zak," Jilly admonished softly.

"I don't want to be married, Jilly. Not to anyone, but certainly not to a woman I don't remember very well who is dying of cancer and wants to give me three kids." He could hear how shallow and selfish he sounded, but this was his life she was talking about!

"That's exactly the point. Crystal is dying. She needs you right now. Don't you think it's terribly, pathetically sad that she has no one else in the world to turn to but a man she's not seen since college?"

Put that way, Crystal's plight looked even worse than it was. And it was bad. "I told her I'd help her. In some way. We can ask at church. Maybe someone will take her in. Maybe someone will want the kids. Or I can hire a nurse to stay with her."

Jilly put a hand on his arm. "I don't know, Zak. Something about that seems wrong to me."

"I can't move her in here. I don't even know her. I have a life, too. What are people going to think if I move a strange woman into my house?"

"What about the kids? Where do they go? What happens to them? They can't care for a dying mother."

He closed his eyes, blew out another breath. "There's the kicker. They have no one to turn to and no place to go."

Jilly bit her bottom lip and he could see the wheels turning inside her head. "Look, all of this has happened too fast. You're reeling from shock. Maybe you need some time to think it over."

"I don't think Crystal has the luxury of time."

"Oh, Zak." She swallowed, pretty face tragic. Jilly was a woman with a heart as big and warm as the sun. She took in all kinds of strays and rejected animals, nursed them to health and found them homes when she could. But three children weren't puppies she could fatten up and farm out. "She's in a desperate situation."

So was he. "I know."

"Can you live with yourself if you don't do something?"

He wished the answer was different but admitted, "I don't know. Probably not. God help me." And he meant that voiced prayer with every cell in his weak brain.

"She's dying, Zak. She must be scared. For herself. For her kids." She squeezed the back of his hand. "I can't imagine how terrible her life must be right now."

"You're killing me."

"I'm trying to put myself in her position. What would I do? What would I need? How hard would it be to ask a near stranger for charity? You can't turn your back. Even if the marriage is on paper only, the two of you are connected. You made a vow to her, even if it was ten years ago. You have an obligation, under God and the law."

Jilly was his best friend. She wouldn't steer him wrong. She wanted the best for him and she wasn't any happier about this than he was, but her head was clearer. His was as tangled as spaghetti. As a Christian, he wanted to do what was right. As a single man, he wanted to jump in his Titan 4x4 and hit the road.

"I can't take on three kids. I won't."

"It's a huge decision."

"Exactly. Those kids need a family. They need someone who wants them and can give them the attention kids deserve. That is not me."

Jilly patted his shoulder. "You're a good guy."

"No, I'm not. I'm struggling."

"You'll do the right thing."

He turned his head to look at her. "Why weren't you around ten years ago to say that?"

She smiled a funny smile. "I wish I had been."

Zak figured he should do some serious knee time, but God hadn't gotten him into this mess in the first place. If he'd been living right back in college, he might have been smarter. Or not. The fact remained, he hadn't been.

"A motel room is no place for a sick woman and a pack of rug rats," he conceded.

"She can't stay there indefinitely, and if she has nowhere to go… You need to find out, Zak. Does she have anywhere else to go?"

"I'll talk to her again."

"And then what?"

He sighed, weary and confused, a load of responsibility bearing down with colossal weight. "I don't know."

As a Christian, his conscience said he had to help Crystal, even though their relationship ended years ago. If helping meant bringing her into his home where she could be at peace for her remaining days, maybe he could do that. But the arrangement was temporary. *Only* temporary.

Maybe, just maybe, a miracle would happen and a family would be found for three orphaned children.

Because he couldn't keep those kids. No matter what.

Chapter Four

Even though Zak spotted Crystal's battered car parked near one of the tidy, flower-rimmed motel units, he stopped at the office first. Call it stalling, call it cowardice, but he wasn't ready to talk to Crystal again. His head was still as muddy as the Redemption River on a rainy day.

The little bell tinkled above the door as he stepped into the cool, rose-scented office, nerves jittery. The blond proprietress, Kitty Wainright Carter, came around a souvenir display counter with a cheerful smile.

Zak spoke first. "You've changed things in here."

The office had once been a memorial to her late war-hero husband. Now, the depressing military shrine had been replaced with whimsical souvenirs of the Oklahoma Land Run and the Old West.

"What do you think?"

"Looks good." A small beagle-type dog came from behind the case to greet him. Zak bent down and scratched the floppy ears. "Hi, Milo."

"Redecorating is fun," Kitty said, "though I'm not doing much of it anymore. Harvey and Faye run the desk for me now full-time. I only came in today to put up the schedule and check on things."

"I heard you were going to sell out."

"We are at some point, but so far, no takers." She widened her eyes and laughed. For a small woman, she had a big laugh. "Imagine that. No one wants to buy a tiny old motel in a small town."

"They don't know what they're missing." He tapped a cowboy bobble head wielding a lasso and watched it flop around. "So how are you feeling?"

Yes, he was doing some serious stalling. Idle conversation with a woman he saw every week at church was easier than offering his home to a dying stranger.

So was jumping off a cliff.

Kitty blushed a pretty pink and patted her barely pregnant belly. "Wonderful."

"How's Jace holding up?" Jace Carter, the local builder she'd married last summer, doted on his wife. Even though Zak didn't get the whole daddy attraction, he recognized Jace as a man who would embrace fatherhood with fear, trepidation and pleasure.

Kitty laughed. "Not nearly as well as I am. He makes at least one trial run to the hospital every day. Yesterday, he had the time down to seven minutes flat." She laughed again. "And I'm only four months along!"

Zak smiled. Jace Carter was quiet and deep, a decent guy who'd loved his wife for years before she knew it. "You'll be great parents."

"I hope so. We're ready. Scared but ready."

He understood the scared part. The ready, not so much. He was an emergency responder, trained to handle stress and to plunge into life-and-death situations. As a pitcher, he could face the toughest batter in the state with bases loaded and nobody out, and blow past him with a curve ball. In the case of Crystal, he was out of his league.

Man up, Ashford.

He shifted, stared at something in the display case called tornado in a can and said, "A woman and three kids checked in today."

Now, *that* was a tornado he wished he could keep in a can.

Kitty nodded. "I noticed her last name was the same as yours. Is she a relative?"

Heat rushed up his back. Crystal had used his name? Right here in the town where he lived and worked and was well respected? Oh, man, what was he going to do if she let the cat out of the bag? He didn't want his friends and neighbors knowing about the dumbest thing he'd ever done.

"Sort of. I saw her car in front of one of the units."

"Unit four. Are you going over there?"

Only if I have to. "Yes. Thanks, Kitty." He pointed at her belly. "Take care."

She laughed her jolly laugh as he exited the building and headed down the path toward Unit Four. The warm afternoon air had suddenly become oppressive and heavy, choking off his oxygen. The overly sweet scent of Kitty's red, white and blue flowers turned his stomach. A black gnat buzzed his nostrils. He swung and missed.

Palms sweaty, he lifted his fist and knocked. From behind the shiny gold number four came the sound of television cartoons.

"Mama, someone's knocking." The raised voice was Brandon's.

Zak didn't hear Crystal's reply but the door opened. Brandon's narrow face peered up at him, serious as a car wreck. The boy swiveled his head toward the inside of the darkened room and said. "He's here, Mama."

A mumble came from Crystal before Brandon opened the door wider and said, "Come in."

Zak controlled the urge to flee. He wasn't a coward,

never had been and he wouldn't start now. He stepped over the threshold and into a small room lit only by the television set. Brandon joined the other two children at the foot of one bed, eyes glued to SpongeBob. Crystal lay on the other, a washcloth draped across her forehead.

The sight made him uncomfortable. He didn't belong in a strange woman's motel room in any capacity other than professional.

Crystal reached for the washcloth, letting it fall to the pillow, and struggled up to one elbow. "Sorry. I'm too tired."

"I can come back another time."

"No." She tried a wan wave of her free hand. "Too tired to get up."

Oh. Pulling his paramedic cloak around him, Zak crossed the short distance to the bedside. "Can I get you anything?"

Her hollow eyes accused. "You know the answer to that."

Zak licked his lips, gone as dry as chalk dust. "That's why I'm here."

She brightened just a bit. "My kids?"

"I can't do that, Crystal, but I can offer you a place to stay while other arrangements are made. I'll help you with those, too. We'll figure out something."

She sighed, eyelids falling shut. Her bird chest rose and fell in a shallow breathing pattern. She was quiet for a while and he wondered if she'd fallen asleep.

Feeling awkward and anxious, pulse drumming in his brain and his inner watchman shouting alarm, Zak glanced at the three children. Engrossed in a fantasy world of television, they seemed oblivious to the fact that their futures hung in the balance. Ignorance was bliss. But he wasn't ignorant.

Finally, Crystal spoke in a weak and whispery voice. "I don't know what else to do."

Grimly, he admitted, "I don't, either."

Zak's wife moved in the next day. Jilly knew this because she'd arrived home from church to find Crystal's car in Zak's driveway and three unsupervised kids playing "kick the can" in the middle of the street.

"Would you look at that? Good lands, Jilly, those kids are going to get killed." Jilly's mother motioned toward the curb. "Pull over. I'm going to give them a talking to."

"Don't get your blood pressure up, Mom. I'll take care of it."

"Who are they and what are they doing at Zak's house? Did he say anything about that woman? Who is she? I hope you haven't fooled around and missed your chance with that cute fireman."

Jilly swallowed back a frustrated reply.

"Mom, this is Zak's business, not mine." She pulled into the driveway, hoping Mom would hurry inside to start Sunday dinner. She hadn't quite decided how to break the news of Zak's marital status.

Mom jerked the straps of her straw bag higher on her arm. "His business will be scraping a child off the pavement if someone doesn't get them out of the street."

"I'll do it." Before her mother could say anything more, Jilly popped her seat belt and hopped out of the car. Traffic in the residential area was light, but Mom had a valid point.

Jilly's heeled sandals poked holes in the damp grass and slowed her progress as she headed down the incline toward the street.

"Tell Zak I'm frying chicken," her mother called. "He's welcome to come over."

Jilly waved a hand. Mom was still trying to reel Zak in with food, but at the moment, her next-door neighbor was in over his head. Impromptu invitations between his house and hers were likely a thing of the past.

The notion settled in her stomach, heavy and dismaying. Zak was married. She'd struggled to sleep last night, had finally gotten up to read her Bible and pray. Considering her prayers were selfish pleas for God to erase the problem, she'd felt worse instead of better.

"Hi, kids," she said as she stepped onto the paved street.

Brandon, the older boy, gave a soup can one more kick before looking at her. The younger boy ignored her to chase the bouncing, rattling can. The little girl—Bella, wasn't it?—had plopped down in the middle of the street to play with rocks. Her face was dirty and if her hair had been brushed this morning, Jilly couldn't tell.

Over the clatter of can against concrete, she asked, "Why don't you play in the backyard?"

Brandon shrugged. "This is better."

She tried a different approach. "Does your mother know you're out here?"

Brandon's face was a mix of disdain and annoyance. "She don't care. She's too busy dying."

Said with such nonchalance, the phrase was obscene. "She does care, Brandon. She's just too sick right now."

His face tightened. "She has cancer."

"I know. I'm sorry." She wanted to put a hand on the boy's thin shoulder but refrained. He didn't seem the snuggly type.

Jake sailed the bent can toward his brother. Jilly stepped in the path to intercept.

"Hey."

"Hey, yourself." She scooped up the can and the little girl. This kid business was harder than she'd imagined, but she knew a thing or two about hurt things. For certain, these kids were hurting. "Come on, let's go inside for a minute."

Brandon shrugged. "Bella's wet anyway."

Jilly had already figured that one out. The evidence sank warm and wet against the side of the peach floral dress she'd bought for Easter. "How old is she?"

"I tree." Bella shoved three short fingers into Jilly's face.

Wasn't three old enough to be out of diapers? She'd have to ask her mom or sister. With two kids, Amber would be up to the minute on toddler parenting.

She gently pushed Bella's fingers out of her face and led the way to Zak's front door. Brandon and Jake went right in. Jilly knocked anyway.

A harried-looking Zak appeared. He pushed the door open. "Hey."

"The troops were on the loose," she said. "In the street. Mom's having apoplexy."

"Sorry. They're like ants, always moving."

Jilly put Bella down. "She's wet."

He rolled his eyes. "Not in my job description."

"If you'll show me where her diapers are, I'll do it."

"Could you?" His relief was evident.

"It's not rocket science, Zak. A diaper's a piece of plastic with sticky tabs. All you have to do is make sure you get the legs tight enough." She made a face. "I learned that the hard way with Amber's boys."

A noise erupted in the kitchen. Zak whirled like a cornered tiger. With Jilly following, he loped into the kitchen.

"Put those down," Zak demanded.

Jake howled like a wolf while he and Brandon wrestled over Zak's Chips Ahoy! They paid no attention to the two adults in the room.

The yowling escalated.

Zak collared them both, one in each strong hand. The arm muscles he'd developed for baseball easily overcame the small boys. "Cut it out, you two. Your mother is asleep."

Brandon dropped the bag. Zak dropped the boys in favor of the cookies. "If you're hungry say so, but don't fight. Just tell me."

Both boys looked stricken. The youngest popped a thumb into his mouth.

"Looks like you've got your hands full." Jilly looked around the messy kitchen. Zak was a neat freak, compliments of his firefighter job. A place for everything and everything in its place. Not so today.

Zak groaned. "Bases loaded. No outs. A-Rod at the plate and my arm is spaghetti."

If she hadn't known Zak for years, she'd be lost in his baseball jargon. But she heard him loud and clear. He was in over his head.

She went to the fridge and pulled out baloney and cheese. "You, kids, go wash your faces and hands. Sandwiches coming up."

The pair dashed out of the kitchen.

Zak wilted against the refrigerator door. "They're here three hours and I'm out of my mind. I can't do this."

She didn't bother to remind him that he already had. "What's the plan?"

"I'm looking for alternatives—anything—but I can't do much until Tuesday. I'm on twenty-four-hour shift tomorrow. Maybe I can make some calls then if we're not too busy. Until then…" He shrugged.

She resisted the urge to offer assistance. This was Zak's situation. He should make the calls. He should decide how all this would play out. "How's Crystal?"

"She's been asleep since they got here." He ran a hand through his hair. "Those kids are wild. They're into everything and they don't bother to ask permission. They do what they want."

"I guess she hasn't had the energy for discipline."

He slid into a chair and banged his head on the tabletop. "I told you I'm not cut out for this."

Bella, sitting on the floor next to the back door, giggled. Jilly patted his back, feeling sorry for him while wondering if she should even be here with a man whose wife was in the other room. Something about that seemed inappropriate. "Mom's making dinner. I have to go."

He lifted his face, looking really pitiful. "Can I go with you?"

Two days ago, she'd have loved that question and would have jumped at the chance to spend Sunday afternoon with him. "Sure."

"Can't. I have to figure out why my life exploded and how to get it back."

She'd known he would say that. Crystal's arrival had changed everything, from Zak's lifestyle to the dynamics of a neighborly friendship.

Finished making three sandwiches, Jilly wiped her hands and started toward the door.

"Aren't you going to change Bella?" Zak's expression was desperate.

"Oh, right. Come here, precious," she said, taking the girl by the hand. Bella's diaper, the plastic dirty from sitting outside, sagged. "Where are the clean diapers?"

He pointed to a plastic shopping bag on the end of the counter. "I made a diaper run this morning. Crystal ran out."

Jilly found the package and worked her magic, thankful for the times she'd babysat her nephews. "We sometimes put diapers on dogs at the clinic. They work just like this.

We use them on squirrels and raccoons, too. Little tiny ones."

Her effort to make him smile failed.

She stood the child on her feet and discarded the soiled diaper. "Don't you have a game today?"

He jerked away from the table, eyes wide. "What time is it?"

"Mom and I stopped at the store after church, so it's probably close to two."

Zak yanked his cell phone from a pocket and glared at the screen. "Oh, man, look at that. Six messages."

Jilly came up behind his chair and leaned in. "Why didn't you hear them ring?"

"Too much going on, I guess." He whopped his forehead with the phone. "How could I forget? This was an important game. I was supposed to pitch."

"Is it too late?"

"Yeah, it's too late. Look at that. Smitty texted me six times."

Jilly read aloud as he scrolled through the texts, one at a time. "Where are you, dude? You're pitching. Are you coming? We're doomed. Taylor's pitching. Batter up. Dude, where are you?"

Zak stroked his left arm. "My arm feels better than it's felt since college. I was so ready. How could I have forgotten?"

She'd watched him last night in his backyard, firing fast balls through the center of a tire hung from a limb of the giant ash tree. He was smoking hot and deadly accurate. She had always wondered why he hadn't made it into the pros.

"Was this a big game?" she asked, aware that any game was important to a baseball junky like Zak. "For a particular reason, I mean."

"Yeah, a tournament in Tulsa." Shoulders stooped, he pushed up from the chair and stared blindly out into the backyard. "The all-star committee is supposed to be there."

Her sympathy gene kicked in. Baseball was the love of Zak's life. In season and out, he lived and breathed it, played and studied it. The dream of playing professionally still lingered.

"The all-star committee?"

"They're putting together a state exhibition team to play around the region. I want on it."

"Was this the last chance?"

"I don't know." He took a milk carton from the fridge, popped open the spout and took a swig. Wearing a milk mustache, he said, "I can't believe I forgot about a game this important."

"You've had a lot on your mind. Once you figure out exactly what's needed with Crystal and the kids, this should get easier."

"I keep telling myself that, but only a few hours in and I think I'm lying." He took another swig of milk. Funny how a guy could do that and look appealing.

The two boys came back in, faces shiny clean. Jilly handed each a sandwich. Baloney in possession, they turned and started toward the living room. Jilly stopped them with a hand on each shoulder. "Sit down at the table to eat, so you don't make a big mess. You want some milk?"

"Oops." Zak looked sheepishly at the milk carton. "Bad habits of a bachelor. You think they'll mind?"

Both boys said "No" at the same time. Jilly figured they never refused anything to eat or drink. She plucked the carton from Zak's fingers and poured each child a glass.

"You're out of milk," she said.

Zak made a face, then lifted Bella onto a chair. Her pixie face barely peeked over the table but both chubby hands reached up and took the halved sandwich. The baloney and bread disappeared below the plane of the table.

Jilly helped Zak put away the sandwich fixings, secretly glad for a reason to linger here with him. When she turned from replacing an unused spoon, he grasped her upper arm. "Thanks."

Her stomach went south. She relished these chance touches just as she relished being this close to him. With effort, she put on her chipper grin, aware that her freckles stood out like beacons when her face wrinkled. "That's what friends are for."

He looked at her long and hard, the strain of the past twenty-four hours evident on his handsome, chiseled features. Jilly, longing to put her arms around him in comfort, settled for a couple of pats to his upper chest. The muscles beneath his white-and-red athletic shirt were rock hard, ready to pitch a fastball or to fight fires. Either way, Zak was in amazing shape. What would it be like to be held in those arms against that chest with his heart beating only for her? For five years she'd wondered.

The sound of movement turned them both to the entry between the living and dining room. A wobbly, wan Crystal, scant hair mussed, entered.

Crystal. Zak's wife.

Jilly's heart sank, a brick in a warm pool. She took one step away from Zak, wishing things were different while knowing all too well, they weren't. And never would be again.

Chapter Five

"What are my options?"

Zak sat in a fancy leather chair across from Hunter Case, attorney at law. Hunter also happened to be a teammate on the local independent baseball team—a crackerjack third baseman with a solid batting average. As such, Zak trusted him with the whole, ugly, painful truth.

"You want me to investigate her claim or do you believe her?" Backlit by the morning sun, Hunter's red hair glowed like a fire around his head. Zak had flashes of Jilly running through his. She'd been a trooper since his life had exploded. Even with her job at the vet clinic, she'd managed to check on Crystal and the kids while he was pulling a twenty-four-hour shift. Her mom, as sympathetic as Jilly, had brought a casserole for the trio of army ants who ate anything in their paths.

His cupboards were bare, his house a mess and he'd missed practice every single night this week.

Three days into his nightmare and he was no closer to waking up than before. It anything, life was harder. The kids weren't mean, but they were undisciplined and confused. They made messes, disappeared without permission and alternately tugged at his heart and infuriated him.

"Both. If she's the same Crystal, she's telling the truth. She never got the divorce. But I need to know for certain where I stand legally."

Hunter scribbled something on a notepad. "What will you do if she's lying? Kick her out?"

Zak blinked. Kick a dying woman out on the street? "I hadn't thought about it."

"You should. If she's falsely using your name and extorting room and board, you could have a case."

"I don't want a case. I want—" He pinched his bottom lip and sighed, frustrated. "I want all this to go away. I want Crystal to be well enough to take care of her kids."

"You're convinced her cancer claims are true?"

Hunter believed the worst in everyone. Suspicion was his job and he did it well. "She saw Dr. Stampley yesterday. He sent for her medical records but told me there was no doubt in his mind of her condition. It's bad, Hunt. Real bad."

"How long did he give her?"

"Days, weeks, months. No one but God knows for sure, but she doesn't have long."

Hunter made a smacking noise. "Bad deal."

Zak found the statement sorely lacking. "Tell me my legal responsibilities." An attorney couldn't help him with the moral dilemma. No one could. Even himself. "Do I have to take those kids? Is the little girl mine just because Crystal gave her my name?"

"*Is* she yours?"

"No! Come on, Hunt. I haven't seen Crystal in ten years."

The lawyer lifted a flat palm. "Had to ask. That's the way it works. I'll have to do some research, but my initial thought is no. You can prove with a paternity test that she is not your biological daughter."

"Yeah." He felt like a creep for asking these questions. "The guys at work are giving me fits."

"Do they know the whole story?"

"They know a woman and a bunch of kids are living at my house. They think I have a live-in." He flexed his pitching hand over and over, keeping his fingers loose out of habit. "I'm a Christian."

"Some Christians do." Hunter pointed a pen at him.

Zak shook his head. "Not this one."

Outside Hunter's second-floor office, the sky was June blue and promised perfect baseball weather. Zak hadn't had time to throw a single pitch in days.

"You could tell people the truth," Hunter said. "The news will probably come out at some point anyway."

A quiver of dread ran through Zak. "I'm not ready for that. The whole stupid mess is embarrassing."

"Everyone has dumb mistakes in their pasts, Zak."

"Even perfect Hunter, heir to the Case fortunes?" The lawyer's family, ancestors of the town's founder, owned this historic building and a lot of other real estate in Redemption.

A tiny muscle twitched beneath one of Hunter's blue eyes. "Money comes with its own stupid mistakes."

While Zak wondered about the statement, he was too focused on his own problems to ask. Hunter wouldn't tell him anyway. If there was one sure thing about Hunter Case, it was his tight lips.

"I feel like the world's biggest loser for worrying about myself when Crystal is dying and her kids are about to be orphans." Zak spread his hands. "But there it is. I wake up in a sweat every morning."

The worry was as much about dealing with Crystal and her brood as saving face.

"You're human. Any man would feel trapped."

Trapped was the right word. He unwound his long length from the cushy chair. "Let me know what you find out?"

"Will do. Meantime, bro, take it easy, don't panic and show up for the next game. We need you." The redhead tossed his gilded pen on the desk. "The Wildcats kicked our tails."

Zak exited the building, the 1900s architectural beauty lost on him. He wanted to telephone his dad in Shawnee, his hometown, for advice, but how could he even begin to explain the situation?

With the warm sun beating on his back and his heart heavy, he crossed the street toward Town Square and the old well dug by the town's founder, Jonas Case. Hunter was descended from the gunslinger-turned-preacher and had intentionally placed his office overlooking the pretty, flowered park that honored his ancestor.

Zak went to the well, a rustic, though still functional structure bearing a plaque placed there by old Jonas himself along with other founding fathers of the town. He absently massaged his pitching arm and read the inscription.

Come unto me all you who labor and are heavy laden and I will give you rest.

"That's me," he murmured. "I'm struggling."

He'd missed church Sunday, but he often did because of his schedule. He and God had things worked out without much church attendance, although he went when he could. Jilly would hound him if he didn't.

There she was in the front of his brain again. She'd acted differently these past few days, almost as if he'd hurt her someway. Oh, she was still Jilly, breezing in and out with her tornadic terriers, but she was different and he missed something about her. He couldn't put his finger on the particulars.

She was disappointed in him. He could tell that much.

And her opinion mattered a lot. He hated disappointing anyone.

Turning from the well, he roamed the small park, watched a couple of kids toss a ball around. He was tempted to jog over and join the game.

Responsibility rushed in. With a wag of his head toward heaven, he headed across the street to the Sugar Shack Bakery and Café. Crystal ate next to nothing. This morning she'd mentioned doughnuts.

The rich, heady scent of baked goods sucked him inside the glass-windowed bakery. The usual regulars sat around shooting the breeze. Behind the counter, bouncy Sassy Carlson and skinny Miriam Martinelli dished out food and conversation. The clamor of voices rose and fell, a pleasant, small-town sound.

He gave his order to Miriam and turned toward the room. Popbottle Jones lifted a hand. "Zak the firefighter, welcome."

Zak wove toward the two most interesting characters in Redemption, Popbottle Jones and GI Jack. Newcomers, him included, frequently mistook the seventy-something pair for bums. Given their unorthodox attire and their habit of scrounging through trash bins for recyclables, the label fit easily, if incorrectly.

"Sit down, son. How you doin'?" GI Jack slid half a piece of toast into his shirt pocket and the other half toward Zak.

"All right, I guess." *I'm drowning. Can't you tell?* He couldn't even enjoy the humor of GI Jack's habit of stocking food in his pockets. "Yourselves?"

"Right as rain," GI Jack answered, head bobbing beneath a green army cap he seldom removed. "Yes, sir, right as rain."

Zak had no more than scooted his chair up to the table

when Popbottle asked, "Heard you had some relatives visiting. A woman and small children, I understand?"

News sailed through a small town, even if the news was only half-correct. "I guess you could say that."

Popbottle's squint was questioning, but Zak had no plan to explain. If rumors wanted to proclaim Crystal a relative, he wasn't about to argue. She *was* a relative, in a manner of speaking.

"I understand the young woman is quite ill. Anything we can do to help?"

They could shoot him. Or take three kids off his hands.

"She has cancer," he said, idly fingering the shared piece of toast. "The docs say her time is running out."

"Yes, so we heard. She's very young." The old professor shook his dignified head. "Tragic."

"And those little kiddies," GI Jack said. "What's to become of them?"

Good question. "I don't know yet."

"Will you keep them, then?"

"Me?" Zak pretended the question was original. "No, not me. But I am trying to find someone who will. Let me know if you hear of a family that might be interested."

Popbottle Jones gave him a long gaze as if he knew something he wasn't telling. "Will do, my boy. Will do."

Sassy hollered from the cash register. "Order's ready, Zak."

He pushed up from the table. GI Jack reached across to reclaim the uneaten toast. Amusement rose in Zak's chest, warm and welcome. "You two take it easy."

At the cash register, he paid and took the white paper bag.

"Miriam put in a few extras for those poor little kids. They like sprinkles, don't they?" Sassy asked, ponytail dancing with the movement of her head.

The baker's generosity lifted Zak's spirit. This was life in Redemption where people cared, one of the reasons he'd felt drawn to the small town after leaving the firefighter's academy.

"Tell her thanks for me, will you?"

Sassy winked. "Sure thing, handsome."

Normally, Sassy's natural inclination to flirt didn't bother him. She joked and bantered with customers all day. Today, it made him feel guilty. He hated that, but there it was. No matter how often he argued that Crystal was not his wife, the obligation rode his back like a two-ton elephant.

Out on the swept-clean sidewalk, doughnut bag giving off a yeasty sweet scent, he listened to the clatter of trash trucks and the hum of citizens going about their business. As he stepped off the curb toward his tricked-out Titan, Jilly pulled in. Her lime-green VW bug bumped the curb and bounced. Dressed in bright blue scrubs and white tennis shoes, she hopped out, heedless of him standing there.

"Hey, neighbor."

She whipped around, red hair swinging around her face, a radiant fire in the sunlight. "Zak!"

Her cheeks blushed in surprise, pink roses under milky skin and a splash of pale chocolate freckles. Milk and chocolate. Couldn't beat that. His insides tickled with gladness. She lived right next door, but seeing her was always a treat.

"Does Dr. Bowman know you're playing hooky from work?" he asked.

"Doughnut run." She grinned. "One of Greg Teague's horses had colic last night and then Barry Kilgore's dad backed over his dog this morning. Trace hasn't had time to look up. So he sent me." Zak knew from talking to the country vet, a good friend, that his practice was bulging at the seams, but Doc Bowman never turned down a needy animal. "Gotta have our sugar fix. What are you doing?"

Guilt came back. "Talking to Hunter Case."

"Oh." She frowned. "About…the situation? Everything okay? How's Crystal this morning?"

He shrugged. "Hard to say. She sleeps a lot."

"Is that because of the illness or the drugs?"

"I don't know." His fist tightened on the paper sack. "Probably both."

"What about her children? Who's watching them?"

"She tells me not to worry about them. Says Brandon is big enough to take care of them."

Jilly bristled, indignant. "No, he's not."

Zak shrugged. He knew next to nothing about kids, but nine seemed a little young to him, too. "That's what I was thinking, but what can I do? They're her kids."

And he wanted them to stay that way. The last thing he wanted was to take responsibility for anyone but himself.

You're a self-centered slob, Ashford.

But he wasn't heartless. "Maybe I should find a nurse or a babysitter or something."

"Have you talked to Annie Hawkins? She does hospice and home health."

Annie was one of Jilly's best friends. "Good idea."

"I could call her if you'd like." She jingled the keys in one hand.

"Would you?" he asked, hopefully, pathetically. He was in such deep water, he was getting the bends.

"Sure. The church is starting Vacation Bible School next week. That could be a temporary option for the children."

Some of the load lifted off his shoulders. "You're a life-saver, Jilly. What would I do without you?"

She gave him a funny little smile and stepped up on the

curb. With the funny smile in place, she disappeared into the Sugar Shack.

Frowning, Zak watched until she was out of sight. There she went again, acting weird. He scratched his head, bewildered.

What was wrong with Jilly?

"What's wrong with you?"

The question came from Amber, Jilly's sister, a brunette with pure skin, classic features and an elegant body. She and matching sister, Nicole, made Jilly feel like a speckled mutt in a kennel of pedigrees.

Jilly cracked the tab of a dog food can and scraped lamb and rice into a bowl for Mugsy and Satchmo. "Nothing. Why?"

Mugsy leaped up, eager for dinner.

"Get back, dog," Amber said, pushing at the terrier with one hand. "How you stand these two idiots on speed is beyond me."

"They're my babies." Jilly set the food bowl on the floor and patted each smiling dog. "Aren't you, precious?"

"You need real babies." Amber pierced her with a sisterly stare, nosy and calculating. Amber, whose own babies were playing at Aunt Nicole's house, had been harping on this topic since the birth of her oldest. "Maybe that's why you're depressed."

"I'm not depressed."

"Yes, you are. And I have a feeling it's because of Zak Ashford."

Depressed was not the word. Disappointed, dismayed and heartbroken, but not depressed.

Their mother sashayed in from watering the plants, bending in the doorway to remove dirty shoes. She set a green spouted can on the cabinet. "Amber's right. You're not yourself since that woman moved in with Zak. What is going on over there anyway? Who is she? A girlfriend? With three kids? I thought Zak was smarter than that."

Jilly tensed. She'd wondered when her family would gang up on her about Zak's houseguests. Even though the truth was bound to come out sooner or later, she'd dreaded the telling.

"Well?" Amber asked. "Who is she? Come on, tell us. I can see by your expression that you know."

The heat on her cheeks was a telltale sign to the whole world. She could not keep her emotions off her face.

"Zak's business—"

"—is obviously yours. You're over there as much as ever. More, I think, and you're acting weird about it."

Jilly sank into a lattice-back chair, the wood worn on the seat's edge. Daddy had sat in this chair.

"Okay, promise you will not tell a soul. At least, not until Zak gives the go-ahead."

Expression rapt, Amber took a celery stick from the fridge and settled across from Jilly. "This sounds intriguing."

"You girls wants some tea?" Mom asked. "I'm parched after being out in that sun."

Both daughters waved her off, so she poured a single glass of amber liquid and sat down, too. "What's going on, Jilly? Talk to Mama."

"And baby sister."

A smile curved Jilly's lips. Her family was the best even if they did nag about her lack of male companionship.

"I was hoping things would work themselves out by now but they haven't. Zak has a…dilemma, I guess you could say." Mugsy raised his paws to her thigh. Out of habit, she absently lifted him to her lap. His tags jingled as he circled once before settling like a cat. She stroked the warm, tricolored fur, glad for the comfort of her pet. "Zak knew Crystal a long time ago in college. Apparently, she has no family so when she got sick she came to him for help."

Jilly knew the explanation lacked the most important truth, but she'd leave out the word "married" if at all possible.

"What's wrong with her?" Amber asked.

"Cancer." Jilly's fingers still on Mugsy's back. "She's terminal."

"Cancer?" Understanding flashed in Amber's blue eyes. She put a hand to her lips. "Like Daddy."

Mom froze, tea glass halfway to her mouth. "I knew she was sick, but not...not...*that.*"

The very word "cancer" struck fear in the hearts of the Fairmont women. Greg Fairmont had died young and fast, a victim of aggressive brain cancer. Like the rest of her family, Jilly remembered the helpless terror of watching their strong father dwindle away in a matter of months.

"Zak is at his wit's end right now trying to figure out what to do."

"Which is no reason for you to spend every spare second over there trying to fix things." Amber gave her celery one hard crunch for emphasis.

Jilly bristled. "I'm being a good neighbor."

"You're being a sap. You're in love with that baseball nut, whether you admit it or not and no matter how many strange women he takes in."

"He's never taken in a strange woman!"

Amber was on a roll and ignored the protest. "And Zak Ashford never paid any attention to you until now. Suddenly, he has a sick woman and a bunch of rowdy kids on his hands, for whatever reason, and there you are. You're too easy. And way too obvious. No wonder he takes advantage."

The words pierced Jilly's heart. She pressed her lips together and got up from the table. Mugsy leaped lightly to the floor but stood, staring up with an equally hurt expression. One minute her sisters were on her case to make a play for Zak and the next they accused her of being too obvious. What they didn't know was that she could do neither. Not anymore.

"Don't be ugly, Amber," Mom said. "I went over there yesterday to take a cake and I saw for myself. Zak needs as much help as he can get. The place was a wreck, the kids messy and pitiful, and Crystal was too sick to do more than say thanks. I should have recognized her symptoms and didn't. Poor thing."

"I just don't like seeing my big sister getting used. Zak isn't stupid. He's bound to know she's crazy for him."

"I'm helping out because I want to, Amber, and because I feel sorry for all of them," Jilly insisted. "Can you imagine what they're going through?"

Amber relented. "At least, if Crystal's sick there isn't any hanky-panky going on between her and Zak. The coast is still clear for you."

"Amber!" Jilly blushed bloodred.

"Well," her sister insisted. "That's what everyone in town is saying about them. No one knows she has cancer. They think she's a live-in."

Jilly groaned. "Great. Poor Zak."

"The truth will soon spread and people will feel terrible for thinking such a thing. That's what gossip causes." Her mom pushed up from the table, put her tea glass in the sink, turning with a determined look on her face. Jilly knew that look. Mom had raised three girls alone on grit and determination. "How can we help, honey?"

"Oh, Mom, I'm not even sure. I talked to Annie about hospice. She's setting that up."

"Hospice can help Crystal but not those children. They don't need a nurse." Mom pressed her lips together. "They need a mother."

"Zak can't take care of them," Amber said. "Not with his work and baseball. I don't know why he doesn't give that up. So juvenile."

Jilly let the comment go. No use getting into an argument by reminding Amber that she and her husband golfed. "I'm trying to find occasional child care to take some of the load. Crystal says she can watch them, but she doesn't."

"What about day care?" Amber asked, reaching in the fridge to tear off another stalk of celery. "You or Mom could drop them off or pick them up."

Jilly shook her head. "Crystal wants them close to her as much as possible. For as long as possible."

"Oh, Jilly." Amber touched her throat. "As a mother, I get that. I can't imagine the worry she's going through. Knowing they need her and too sick to provide care."

"Plus, she knows her time is short and they'll have no one."

The bare truth brought silence to the kitchen. The ticking clock reminded Jilly that time was passing and with it, Crystal's life.

"Surely, we can do something." Mom pressed her lips together, thinking. After a few seconds, she patted Jilly's hand. "You're right, honey. We're supposed to treat our neighbors as ourselves and if that poor woman is in need, we should at least offer. Do you suppose she'd let me watch the little girl some? I have quite a bit of experience with little girls, you know, and I'm right next door."

"Oh, Mom, would you? If nothing else, could you help me potty train her? I told Crystal I'd try to do it, but you're an expert. Crystal is too sick, and Zak is clueless."

"That's not a man's job anyway." Mom opened a cabinet and dragged out the food processor.

"Don't be sexist, Mother." Amber crunched the celery. "Men do lots of things today that Daddy didn't do."

"Well, still." Mom slammed a cabinet door and plopped the food processor on the counter with a determined smack. "That's my opinion."

"You need your summer break to recuperate," Amber said. Mother was a teacher's aide at the local high school. "With your health, are you sure you're up to dealing with a toddler?"

"I need to do something around here besides cook and eat. My blood pressure has gone up instead of down."

Not to mention her sugar.

Jilly leaned in for a quick hug. "Thank you, Mom. I'll ask Crystal, but I'm sure she'll agree. Bella needs someone like you."

"Amber, be useful," Mom said over one shoulder. "Get the apples and celery out. You've made me hungry for Waldorf salad."

"People say she is Zak's ex-wife." Amber plopped two green apples and a bag of celery on the counter. "I didn't know he'd been married."

"She's not his ex," Jilly said before she could think.

"No? You're telling me Zak is such a soft touch he just allows random acquaintances to move into his house?"

Jilly swallowed, wishing she'd kept her mouth shut. "You'll have to ask Zak."

Amber's fingers grasped Jilly's upper arm and squeezed. "I'm your sister. If you know what's going on, you have to tell me. Everyone in town is talking. Who is that woman and why is she living with Zak?"

Jilly gazed from her sister to her mother and thought she

would explode if she didn't share her hurt with someone. This was family, people who loved her.

"She's not his ex." She took a deep breath and blurted, "She's his wife."

Chapter Six

The news was all over town by the end of the week. Zak vacillated between trying to explain and trying to avoid the subject of his college indiscretion. The guys at work were giving him fits. Even the pastor had stopped in for a talk. The bottom line was, he had a responsibility to a woman he'd once married, and he was man enough to face it. He didn't like it but he was coping. Sort of.

He slid a hand into his Mizuno Pro baseball glove and flexed the fingers, held the leather to his nose and inhaled. Even the smell of the game relaxed him. As a boy, he'd slept with a battered old Wilson under his pillow and dreamed of pitching in Yankee Stadium.

As a man, he still dreamed.

He exited his bedroom, the only sanctuary he could find from the overwhelming noise and clutter and sickness, only to discover little Jake standing outside the door, thumb in his mouth. Zak was still startled to find other people living in his house. He couldn't help resent the intrusion.

"Hi, Jake." He forced himself to ruffle the boy's dark hair. None of this was the kids' fault.

Jake observed him with dark, questioning eyes. He was

a sad little dude who cried a lot. Zak didn't know what to do with him.

"Can I go?"

Zak didn't pretend not to understand. Even a six-year-old recognized a baseball uniform when he saw one.

Zak ran his free hand down the front of the red-and-blue jersey. Number sixteen, the great Yankee southpaw Whitey Ford's retired number. "I don't know, Jake. There's no one to look after you while I play."

"Brandon."

Zak rotated the worn baseball in the fingers of his left hand. The feel was good today. He had his stuff.

"No, not Brandon."

Tears sprang to the boy's eyes. Zak searched for a quick solution before Jake started to howl. From experience, he knew that Jake's howls, once started, were not easily stopped.

"Hey, don't cry now." He patted the kid's shoulder with his gloved hand. "Maybe Jilly can come with us."

"Jilly?" the boy asked hopefully.

"Yeah, Jilly. Wanna give her a call?" A tweak of guilt pinched at him. Jilly had a life. Maybe he expected too much of his easygoing neighbor, but he hoped she'd come. He'd missed three games since that fateful Saturday. Three! How could he make the all-star squad if he didn't pitch? And he missed hanging out with Jilly. She'd understand. She always did. And she liked coming to his games. At least, she used to.

He dug his phone from his pocket and punched Jilly's speed dial. Two minutes later, with relief flooding through him as if he'd just struck out the last batter with bases loaded, Zak slapped Jake a high five. "Wash your face and change your shirt. Where's Brandon?"

Jake shrugged and disappeared down the hall to the

room he shared with his two siblings, once Zak's game room. Crystal had taken the guest room next to her children. Zak still felt awkward about the arrangement but made a point of informing Crystal when he left the house. He headed there, knocked softly and waited for her, "Come in."

Even though this was his house, he stood in the entrance, uncomfortable. The television set at the end of the bed was on low, the movement flickering in the dim room. Crystal was propped high on several pillows. At her side, someone—Jilly, he thought—had arranged a table with essentials. Medication, a water bottle and a banana along with books and girly stuff that Crystal mostly ignored, too weak to bother with anything but the medication. The fingernails of only one hand were painted cherry red, a half manicure from Jilly that ended when Crystal fell asleep. The banana, he noted, was turning black. Did she ever eat anything?

"I have a ball game. Jilly's coming, too. She'll watch the kids if it's okay with you."

A ghostly smile stretched Crystal's paper thin lips. She'd grown more emaciated with each passing day, and the scent of sickness hovered in the air. He hated coming in this room, hated seeing the once-charming, bubbly girl reduced to this by a hideous disease, hated the overwhelming responsibility.

"Your neighbors are nice. You're lucky."

He didn't feel so lucky.

He tossed the ball into his glove and swallowed. "You need anything?"

"Nothing you can provide. Go on."

She knew he chaffed against the restraints her arrival had put on him. She also knew he avoided her, another reason to feel guilty. Crystal made him feel many things, none of them positive. Resentment, guilt, anger, self-pity.

He wanted his life back.

With a start, he realized, Crystal wanted hers back, too.

Crowded into Zak's truck with three kids and two dogs on the bench seat in the back and a pile of baseball equipment between her and the driver, Jilly wondered why she'd agreed to play babysitter. Mom had given her grief. Being seen with a married man ranked high on Mom's no-no list. The thought made Jilly uncomfortable, although she'd reminded her mother that she was only the babysitter. The word had tasted like ashes.

"Rough day at work?" he asked, looking from the steering wheel to Jilly.

"Same as always."

"You're quiet. Everything okay?"

Men could be such idiots. She wanted to bop him on the head and say, "No, dummy, I love you. And you're married. I feel guilty and irrationally hurt."

Instead she said, "Fine. How about you? The guys at work still bugging you?"

"Not as much. Once they found out about Crystal's illness, they shut up."

"That's the only good use of a cancer diagnosis I can think of."

"Me, too." He sighed, the weight of all he was dealing with evident in the sound. He hadn't been his usual happy-go-lucky self in a while now, either.

In the backseat, the kids watched a movie on the DVD player Zak had purchased for that purpose. He was kind to Crystal's children. He'd make a good father, whether he knew it or not.

The thought pierced her through, like a hot needle. She'd entertained the notion of his being a father someday, but not to someone else's children.

She turned her face to the window and stared out at the passing town. Redemption's picture-postcard beauty drifted by, bright fragrant flowers on green lawns and stately old homes that evoked a feel of elegant nostalgia.

People said Redemption drew the lost and the hurting. She wondered if that was true in Crystal's case. If God had somehow led her to Redemption, He must have a plan. Jilly wished she knew what it was.

They drove down Mercy Street, past the vet clinic where she worked and onward toward the sports complex on the edge of town.

She wanted to question Zak, to ascertain his thoughts and plans, to know if Hunter Case had discovered any useful information on the divorce, or if anyone had stepped forward about the trio of children. The words stuck in her throat, held there by the ugly knowledge that asking seemed cruel, as if she wished Crystal dead.

"We fought a grass fire yesterday out by Ted Sikes's place," Zak said, breaking through the background noise of Disney.

Jilly turned back to face him, glad for normal conversation, the things they always talked about. Her mind couldn't seem to focus on anything but the situation. "Was it bad?"

"Bad enough. We got there in time to protect the house and chicken coop, but he lost some fence and a lot of pasture land." They neared the sports complex, and Zak clicked on his blinker. "If we don't get rain, we'll see a lot more."

Drought this time of year wasn't that unusual and with frequent wind and miles of grassland surrounding Redemption, fires were a real danger. "You'd think the burn ban would help."

"It does, but people still want to burn trash or flip cigarettes out the car window." The truck eased to a stop next to a tall fence surrounding the ballpark. "Here we are." He rotated his shoulders. "Man, it's good to be back."

She snorted. "You missed three games, Zak, not the whole season."

"Felt like forever." Keys jingling, he hopped out and opened the back door for the kids, helping first Jake and then Bella to the long step down. When he reached for Brandon, the boy shifted away and jumped down by himself. Zak and Jilly exchanged glances. Brandon was aloof and moody.

"I've got them, Zak. Go on. You're dying to get out there."

His grin was her reward. "Thanks, Jilly. You're a lifesaver."

How many times had he said that lately? She watched him lope toward his welcoming teammates. The other players clapped him on the back, their grins saying they were as happy to have him back as he was to be there. The boys of summer. The term fit Zak and his friends perfectly.

"Can I have a hot dog?"

Jilly looked down into Brandon's closed face. What would it take to get inside the child's head? Only nine and yet he held back, unwilling or unable to let anyone close. "Have any of you eaten?"

The smell from the concession was enough to make anyone hungry for popcorn and a hot dog.

The boys answered at once, although their replies conflicted. "Yes. No."

Brandon whacked Jake on the side of the head. The younger brother broke into a loud cry. Bella plopped down in the dirt and already had a handful on her clothes.

"Boys, boys! Stop it. No hitting and no crying." She grabbed Bella and stood her up. Wrestling a Great Dane into a bath was easier than dealing with these kids. "If you want a hot dog, you can have one—as long as you don't cry or fight about it."

Jake stuck his thumb in his mouth. Tears rolled down his cheeks, but he stopped the loud crying and sniffled. Face closed, Brandon said nothing. Jilly felt helpless to reach the older boy. She knew he had to be hurting, but he seemed so distant.

"Come on. The concession is over by the bathrooms. Bella, you need to go potty?"

Bella smiled, a mischievous twinkle in her blue eyes. Better make a pit stop for everyone. The toddler was picking up potty training fairly quickly, thanks to Mom, but she was stubborn and ornery, too.

After bathroom and concession, with hands full of ball field junk food, they headed toward the stands, choosing a place immediately behind the backstop for a good view of the pitcher's mound. Mugsy and Satchmo, accustomed to the routine, hopped up the metal steps, toenails *click-clicking*. A half dozen hands reached out to pat as the friendly duo passed.

When the game commenced, Jilly's heart thrilled at watching Zak stride out to the mound for warm-up. With his lanky form and easygoing, confident smile, he looked handsome and powerful and in control, a mighty pitcher for the Redemption Rogues.

"Zak, Zak, Zak!" Bella and Jake bounced on the bleachers, jiggling Cokes and threatening spills. Zak, bless him, lifted his glove in their direction and grinned. Jilly knew the greeting was for the kids, but her stomach quivered anyway. She wiggled her fingers at him, unreasonably thrilled.

Even if he wasn't animated, Brandon had his brown gaze on the rangy pitcher. The child needed a hero to adore and

Zak, whether he knew it or not, had been chosen. Brandon watched his every move.

There was a sweet and hurting child inside the aloof little personality. He was kind to Bella and Jake most of the time, or at least tolerant, caring for them like a miniature adult, and he was, at the moment, sneaking bites of hot dog to each of the terriers.

Zak smoked his fastball past the first three batters and retired the side quickly, much to the delight of his team-mates and the home crowd. As the Redemption Rogues jogged toward the dugout, Brandon asked, "Can I go talk to Zak?"

Considering this was the first time he'd asked permission to do anything, she said yes.

"Batter up!"

The Rogue's lead-off batter was Hunter Case. On the third pitch, an inside curve, he tilted his body inward and took the pitch on the meat of his shoulder. With a jaunty grin as if he'd done it on purpose, he tossed his bat aside and jogged to first base.

Jilly whooped and hollered with the rest of the crowd. The lawyer always had a trick up his sleeve. Once on first, he flapped his arms, threatened to steal second and gener-ally annoyed the opposing pitcher as much as possible.

Jilly glanced toward the dugout to see Zak leaning over the metal bar, one sleeve of a jacket on his pitching arm and a wide grin on his face. He was never more handsome or alive than when here on the field. He clapped his hands and yelled encouragement to Hunter. She did the same.

A trio of new arrivals started up the bleachers, blocking her view. She recognized the group as friends and looked up with a smile of greeting. Kade McKendrick and his ad-opted son, Davey, along with fiancée, Sophie Bartholomew, scooted in next to her. Mugsy stuck his head under Sophie's hand for a rub. The terriers refused to be ignored.

"I know *these* little guys," Sophie said, patting Mugsy first and then Satchmo. Jake reached out and drew Satchmo back as though the dog was his. "But who are your new friends?"

Jilly introduced the two children who simply gazed at the pretty brunette with interest. "These are Zak's house-guests."

"We heard something about that in church, didn't we, Kade?" Sophie placed a hand on Jilly's arm and murmured softly. "How is their mother?"

In the same quiet undertone, Jilly shook her head and said, "Not well."

Kade added, "If we can do anything..."

Warmth flooded Jilly. She'd been sitting here, all tensed up, afraid they'd ask about Zak and Crystal's marriage. Instead, these kind hearts showed concern. "Thank you. I'll tell Zak you offered. I know he'll appreciate it."

"Anything, anytime." Sophie reached one hand toward Jilly. "You know I mean that." Her engagement ring flashed in the sunlight.

Jilly's eyes widened. "Wow, Sophie, let me see your ring."

With a big smile characteristic of the schoolteacher, Sophie extended her hand in pride and joy. "Kade bought it in Chicago when we went to meet his family."

Gladness and envy warred inside Jilly. Would she ever wear an engagement ring? "This is gorgeous. When's the wedding?"

Sophie's dark hair swung against her white blouse as she cast a besotted gaze toward Kade. "We're thinking October in the Hawkinses' Wedding Garden."

The darkly handsome cop grinned, his brown eyes alive

with love for Sophie. "Unless I can convince her to elope sooner."

Sophie laughed and squeezed his hand. The display of love was almost more than Jilly could take. Even though glad for her friends, her heart ached for a love of her own.

She glanced toward the dugout, saw him there, grinning, lanky, affable. One of the true good guys. Why did he have to be someone else's husband?

A bat cracked and cheers erupted from the opposing fans. Rogue fans groaned. All three adults turned attention to the field to see Hunter Case trotting off the field amid a swirl of dust, thrown out trying to take third on a single.

"Get 'em next time, Hunt," Jilly yelled. Then, to her friend, she said, "The gardens will be beautiful that time of year."

"That's what we thought, and Davey's voice should be healed by then." Sophie put an arm around the blue-eyed boy beside her.

Kade, sitting with clasped hands dangling between his knees spoke to Davey. "Gotta get that voice in shape to read a certain Psalm, right, buddy?"

"Yes, Dad." The towheaded Davey's voice was hoarse, a result of years of unuse. Surgery for a congenital defect a few weeks ago had given him his first spoken words. According to Sophie, Davey was a walking—and now talking—miracle.

Jilly considered the child, about Brandon's age and wondered if the pair could be friends.

She glanced toward the dugout and spotted Zak, preparing to take the mound again. Brandon was not there.

"Did either of you see where Brandon went?" she asked of Jake and Bella.

The pair shook their heads. Bella batted blue eyes. "I gotta go baffroom."

Jilly and Sophie exchanged amused looks.

"We'll keep an eye on Jake," Sophie said. "You take Bella and go."

Glad for the assistance, Jilly said, "If Brandon gets back before I do, tell him to stay put. Okay?"

Jake nodded and snuggled the older, calmer Satchmo closer. Hyperactive Mugsy refused to be left behind and trotted down the metal bleachers with Jilly and Bella.

When they returned, Brandon was still unaccounted for.

"He's probably behind the stands playing with some of the kids who gather back there," Sophie said.

A teacher would know more about kid habits than Jilly. "That makes sense. I'll run down and check."

He wasn't there, either.

Worry started to set in. Where was he? She scanned the area around the baseball field and surrounding stands in search of a dark-haired boy in a bright blue shirt. As usual, the place was crowded and a nine-year-old could be obscured from view by someone taller.

Leaving Bella and Jake with Sophie, she walked to the concession and around behind the dugouts. Out on the field, Zak was cutting down batters with surgical precision. The crowd was in it, screaming his name and whooping like mad each time the umpire rang up another strike. He had a rhythm going, pitching as well as she'd seen him pitch. She wanted to share the moment.

Surely, Brandon would reappear soon.

Her stomach jittered with worry. Brandon had a habit of doing his own thing and occasionally wandered off without telling anyone. But today, she was responsible, and he was just a little boy. If anything happened to him…

She drew in a shaky breath, steadying herself. Nothing was going to happen. He was here somewhere.

Maybe she should ask Zak when he came off the field.

About that time, the umpire yelled, "Strike three!"

The Redemption crowd roared as Zak and his teammates jogged toward the dugout. Jilly headed that direction, too.

When she approached, the catcher, still in chest and knee gear, pounded Zak on the back. All the players were smiling and exchanging congratulatory fist bumps. She wished she could celebrate with him.

"Zak."

He whipped around, face sweaty and green eyes alight with positive energy. He raised his hand for a high five. She smacked his long, talented fingers with hers.

"Did you see that last batter? That's Tim Rogers, regional home run king. Fastball, fastball, change-up and he's out of there!" He pumped his arm in imitation of the ump.

"Awesome," she said, dreading to ruin his good time.

"You're getting pink." He stuck his sweaty ball cap on her head. "How are the rug rats doing? Any problems?"

"Is Brandon over here with you?"

"Was." He swiped the back of his wrist over a forehead creased with a band of sweat and dirt. "I gave him money for sunflower seeds. Why?"

"He never came back."

Zak's jubilation dissipated. "That was first inning."

"I can't find him."

He shrugged his left arm into a jacket. "You looked everywhere?"

She nodded. The bill of his cap slid farther down her forehead. The essence of Zak, sweaty and salty and masculine enveloped her in a false sense of possession. The thought struck her that even wearing his ball cap possibly crossed a line of right and wrong. Even though he wasn't hers, she wanted him to be. She could never feel sisterly about Zak.

Troubled by more than the missing boy, she said, "I

walked the grounds, looked behind the bleachers, yelled into the bathrooms, everywhere I could think of."

A struggle, fast and decisive, took place behind Zak's spiky black eyelashes.

"Give me a minute." He spun around, stalked to the end of the dugout and looked out, scanning the area as she'd done. Sweat patched the back of his blue uniform shirt, setting the red number sixteen in relief. After a brief look, he barked, "Coach, take me out."

The sixty-something coach, salt-and-pepper hair poking from beneath his Rogue ball cap, protested in disbelief. "What are you talking about, Ashford? You've got a no-hitter working."

"Take me out. I'm done." The line of Zak's jaw was grim, a stark contrast to moments before.

Jilly hurt for him. Baseball was his passion. He lived for days like this when all the elements aligned for a perfect game.

With a beleaguered sigh, Coach Branson yanked the clipboard from its nail and yelled, "Starks, warm up. Ashford's done."

Murmurs of protest spun through the dugout, but Zak ignored them. If Jilly hadn't loved him before, she'd have fallen madly at that moment. For all his argument about not being the right man to care for those kids, when they needed him, he was willing to give up the thing he loved most to come to their aid.

Who wouldn't love a man like that?

"I can find him, Zak," she said quietly, going to his side. She removed his cap and held it out to him. "Finish your game."

He crammed the blue cap down over sweat-drenched

hair. The red Rogue insignia smiled out with bared teeth. "Let's go."

Without waiting, he charged out of the dugout and began to search, leaving behind a six-zero lead and a no-hitter.

Chapter Seven

Jake cried and sucked his thumb. Bella whined and clung to Jilly's hand. Zak envied them both. Torn between disappointment at leaving the game and worry about Brandon, he moved the little family past the bleachers, searching. Spectators called out. He lifted a hand, wishing he had time to revel in today's game but focused on finding a troublesome nine-year-old. Crystal had enough on her plate without something happening to one of her kids.

"He can't be far," Jilly said. Skin pink from sun and exertion, her freckles stood at attention. If not for Brandon, he would have teased her. "I'm really sorry."

"Not your fault. He pulls the disappearing act at least once a day." The gloomy kid was driving him nuts.

"Where does he go?"

"Nowhere, he says." Zak shrugged. "He's a boy. Probably gets distracted by something. I saw him messing with your rabbits one day."

Jilly's bow mouth formed an O. "I didn't know that."

She resembled a pixie. A really cute, red-haired pixie. His insides smiled, and he had the strangest desire to keep right on looking at his next-door neighbor. Not that she was hard to look at. Never had been. In modest white shorts and Rogue blue tee, she looked…hot.

Whoa. Whoa! Where had that come from? This was Jilly, his next-door neighbor, his best pal.

He yanked his gaze away and cleared his throat. "I told him to stay out of your backyard."

"Maybe I should invite him over and teach him some rabbitology."

No wonder he liked her. "First we have to find him."

Kade McKendrick suddenly appeared around the corner of a building, one hand on a boy's shoulder, guiding him. It was Brandon.

Zak didn't even know Kade, a special assistant to the local sheriff, had joined the search. But he was grateful.

Zak and Jilly rushed to the pair. Jake flung both arms around his brother and wailed. Bella wet herself.

"Kade, man, thank you." Zak offered a sweaty palm.

Kade took the offered hand in a quick, modern exchange—more a sideways squeeze than a handshake. "Glad to help."

"Where was he? What was he doing?"

Kade, whose aloof, secretive personality was perfect for his former DEA job, squeezed Brandon's shoulder. "I'll let him tell you." And then with a half smile, he melted back into the crowd toward his waiting fiancée.

As though his brother, now found, was mortally wounded, Jake's cries escalated. People turned to stare. Zak's head started to ache. The heat, unnoticeable when he was on the mound, bore down like a furnace.

Jilly gently pried the smaller boy off his brother. "Hush, Jake. Brandon is fine."

Yeah, Brandon was fine now, but the little twerp might not be when Zak got through with him. A few weeks into this ordeal and the antics were starting to wear thin. If

Hunter Case didn't find something soon... Zak let the thought go. Brandon was the issue now, not Zak's ill-advised marriage.

He gave Jake a hard-eyed stare, the kind he used on batters to intimidate. The howler sniffed to a shuddering stop and stuck his thumb in his mouth. That was another thing that annoyed him. Why was a six-year-old sucking his thumb? And why was Bella always wet?

With back teeth tight enough to require the Jaws of Life, Zak narrowed his eyes and said to Brandon, "Talk. Where did you go? Why didn't you tell Jilly or me?"

Brandon wasn't intimidated. He mumbled, "I don't know."

Zak's patience was about to snap. He, a laid-back guy, was being pushed to the limit by a trio of rug rats. "You better figure it out real fast."

Jilly laid a hand on Zak's arm. Quietly, she said, "Zak left the ball game to look for you. He was pitching well, but now he can't go back in the game. Do you understand that we were worried about you because we care?"

Brandon's sullen expression softened. He stared at his untied shoelace. "I was just walking around. Baseball's boring."

"Boring?" Zak couldn't believe his ears. *Boring?* What was wrong with this kid? "You ever played?"

Brandon's shoulder hitched. "No. It costs money and Mama don't have none."

Zak's anger softened like the black grease under an outfielder's eyes in the blazing sun. With Crystal for a mother, Brandon probably hadn't done much of anything but take care of his siblings.

Even though the kid tended to shy away from physical touch, Zak eased a hand onto his shoulder. More gently this time, he asked, "Wanna learn?"

Brandon shrugged again, loosening Zak's grip, but his head came up and his dark eyes searched Zak's, asking if the offer was real. Zak's gut clenched to think a nine-year-old could already be cynical.

"I wanna play," Jake said with a big sniff. His nose was runny from crying, but at least his thumb wasn't in his mouth. It was wet and wrinkled, but disconnected from his face.

"I want to pitch like Zak." The skinny six-year-old whirled his arm round and round.

Brandon rolled his eyes at his brother's antics but said, "Can I bat first?"

Behind them, a groan went up from the crowd. Zak spun toward the sound, scanning the field and the scoreboard in one fast read. His heart dropped to his cleats. There went his no-hitter.

Man. He wanted back in that game. He shifted, his cleats scraping sand. He loved that sound.

A bat connected with a ball, the crack of a high fly, a pitcher's promise of a sure out. He loved that sound, too.

But for today, for him, the game was over.

"Ready to go home?" he asked, quietly, regretfully.

"Are you kidding? No way." Jilly punched his arm. "The Rogues need us."

He was tempted to hug her. She knew what this game meant to him.

Rubbing the spot where her small fist had made friendly contact, he did that staring thing again, noticing things about Jilly he'd taken for granted for so long. She was special, his next-door neighbor.

He stuck his cap on her head and tugged it down over laughing blue eyes. The urge to hug her came again, only this time the feeling was anything but neighborly.

What was the matter with him today?

He blew out a breath and turned toward the dugout to sit with the players. Then just as suddenly as the hug urge had hit, he did a one-eighty. Sitting in the bleachers with Jilly and the rug rats sounded better.

A siren pierced the air, louder than the cheers of the spectators. Heads swiveled toward the sound, although Zak recognized the siren and the direction. Fire and rescue. The rhythm of his pulse picked up the way it did every time the alarm came in.

His trained eyes scanned the sky and caught a puff of smoke. His heart lurched. The blaze wasn't far away.

Zak had been called in at midnight to help fight the enormous fire that, aided by wind and drought, had raced through the pasture land less than a mile from the ballpark. Several horses and cows had been affected, but thankfully no homes or lives were lost. When Jilly arrived home after an exhausting day of assisting Dr. Bowman with the animal casualties, Zak's truck was not in his driveway.

She and Mom ate dinner. She fed the dogs and rabbits, tired but restless. Zak's drive remained empty except for Crystal's beat-up Chevy, which hadn't been moved since her arrival. Was Zak still working?

"Everyone at the clinic was talking about the fires we're having," she said as she rubbed a white plate shiny with a dish towel. They had a dishwasher but Mom refused to use it, saying a sink saved water and money and got the dishes cleaner. "Yesterday's was the worst so far."

"Happens nearly every year." Mom shouldered a lock of dark blond hair from her cheek. Bent over the sink with spatula in hand and an apron around her waist, she reminded Jilly of a slightly overweight version of Meryl Streep. Mom, like Nicole and Amber, was a beautiful woman.

"This year seems worse. Mrs. Pearson brought in her blue heeler. He burned his pads trying to move the cattle to safer pasture."

"Poor dog."

"She thinks someone is intentionally setting the fires."

"Oh, honey, I hope not." Mom yanked the stopper on the sink. The water guzzled down the drain. "What does Zak say about that?"

"Haven't talked to him. I guess he's still working." She handed Mom her towel. "Have you noticed the nurse's car over there today?"

Her mother dried her hands and hung the dish towel over the oven door, frowning. "Not that I recall, but I could have missed it. Bella was here for most of the morning."

Which meant Jake and Brandon had roamed free all day with only a sick woman to care for them.

Jilly put away the last dish and closed the cabinet with a soft thud. "Maybe I should go over and make sure the kids are fed."

"Jilly, you do too much for them already." Mom folded the apron in half and then in half again, smoothing the well-washed flowered material with hands beginning to show signs of age. "None of us mind lending a hand, but ultimately they're Zak's responsibility, not yours."

The children weren't Zak's biologically, but convincing her mother and sisters of that fact was hopeless. "They need me."

The hands paused. Mom pierced her with a look. "The children or Zak?"

Jilly bit her lip. "Both. All of them. They're going through a difficult time."

And so was she, although her family didn't know or understand.

"Zak's *wife* has a nurse. The church is helping. I'm helping. I thought we settled that."

Jilly flinched at the phrasing. No one needed to remind her that Crystal and Zak remained married. "That's different."

Diane placed the apron on the counter with a sigh. "Honey, for your own good, you should back off before everyone in town gossips about you for chasing after a married man. You know how rumors fly in a small community, and this does not look good."

Jilly stiffened. "Mom, that is so not fair!" Satchmo, cruising the floor for leftovers, looked up at the distress in his owner's voice. "I'm not chasing him."

"Oh?" Mom cocked her head to one side in that way mothers do when they are about to shoot a zinger. Jilly braced for it. "Then explain why, when he called yesterday, you skipped out on a *planned* dinner with Nicole and Rich. And then sprinted across the street to his house faster than one of these terriers? Face it, honey, your frequent visits have nothing to do with philanthropy. Please, for your own sake, don't be pathetic."

Without another word, Jilly whirled and marched out of the kitchen. Mom and the sisters made a habit of pointing out her weaknesses. With her heart and her conscience already struggling over the situation next door *and* her feelings for Zak, she didn't need the additional grief.

As she reached the front door, her mother's voice called, "Read the tenth commandment."

Jilly yanked open the door with enough force to rip the hinges loose and fled down the steps, leaving behind the surprised terriers. She didn't have to look up the scripture to know which one it was. The one mom always tossed out whenever Jilly, Nicole or Amber wanted something their friends had and Mom didn't have the money.

Thou shalt not covet.

She strode down the grassy incline, pausing at the curb leading onto the quiet street. She'd prayed about her feelings for days, asked God to take them away. She didn't want to be guilty of breaking a commandment.

With a glance upward toward June skies—an ocean of blueberry jelly dappled with fluffy, marshmallow clouds—she wondered why God answered some prayers and not others.

By the time she was inside Zak's living room, the tight cord of tension in her neck had reached the snapping point.

To make matters worse, Zak's house was a wreck. Zak liked a place for everything and everything in its place, a natural outcropping from his work at the fire department. Having messy, undisciplined kids underfoot day and night must be driving him crazy. No wonder he hadn't come home yet.

Food wrappers, half-eaten bowls of cereal and a drippy glob of jelly decimated the once-nice leather ottoman table. A pink crayon was crushed into the brown carpet and the dollar store toys the church had sent over lay scattered everywhere. The television was on, as always, but without a viewer.

The neck tension worked its way between her shoulder blades. She waded through the disaster—the aftermath of a tornado—to pick up the pieces.

From somewhere came the sound of running water. She paused with bowls and cups in hand to listen, visions of flooded rooms and bathtub drownings in her head. The sound seemed to be coming from the bathroom, so after depositing the dishes in the kitchen, she threaded her way down the hall.

The bathroom door stood open. Crystal leaned over the sink, splashing water on her ashen face.

Feeling intrusive, Jilly hesitated near the door.

Crystal pushed back from the sink and swayed.

"Crystal?" Without waiting for an invitation, Jilly stepped inside to steady the sick woman. "Are you okay? Can I do something for you?"

A trembling hand reached toward the towel bar. Jilly grabbed the hand towel and placed it in Crystal's fingers. "Let's get you back to bed. Okay?"

Crystal nodded, her chest rising and falling in short, quick gasps. Quivers ran through her emaciated body. Jilly slid an arm around her waist, aware of the sharp contrast between her healthy, strong body and Crystal's quickly fading one. Pity welled in her throat.

After a slow, agonizing journey in which Crystal paused numerous times to catch her breath, she settled into bed and closed her eyes. The smell of sickness in the room was cloying.

"Should I call the nurse?"

Crystal shook her head, a scratchy sound against the white pillow case.

"Do you know where the kids are?" Odd that she should be asking instead of the children's mother.

"Zak took them to buy ball gloves." Crystal moistened dry lips and looked toward a cup of water that sat on the nearby table. "Would you mind? A pill, too."

Jilly shook out a pain pill, then held the straw to the other woman's lips. Crystal gulped down the water and medication and then fell back, panting.

"Ball gloves?"

Crystal nodded. "He's been real good to them."

Zak's actions touched a chord inside Jilly. He had been up for thirty hours or more, and yet he'd remembered his promise to teach the boys about baseball.

Oh, Zak, no wonder I love you so much.

The thought rushed in with the flood of warmth to her soul, a shaft of sunlight and sweetness. Just as quickly, guilt followed. She glanced at the woman on the bed, eyes closed, the pulse above her protruding collar bone as rapid as the wings of a hummingbird. Crystal was dying, not by small increments but in huge gulps.

Thou shalt not covet.

Crystal's eyelids fluttered open. "You love him."

Jilly tried not to react, tried to keep the truth from her face and her answer. "He's married."

"Never stopped *me* from going after a guy." Crystal gave a short laugh that ended in a pained cough. "Look where that got me."

"Crystal…" Jilly didn't know what to say.

She lifted a feeble hand from the blue sheets. "Hey, it's okay. I made my own mistakes. No one to blame but me."

Try as she might, Jilly couldn't keep from asking, "Was Zak a mistake?"

The medication began to do its work and Crystal's eyes glazed, her lids drooping. "Zak. Only smart thing I ever did. Except raise my kids." Her eyes widened then, and the shrinking pupils gleamed, frantic. Her bony fingers reached toward Jilly, grasping, pleading. "My kids. Make him promise."

Jilly took the fragile hand in hers, searching for the right words. Before she could find them, Crystal's eyelids fell shut and her body relaxed. The powerful medication had taken hold.

Still holding the frightfully frail hand, Jilly settled in a chair beside the bed, watched until the pinched skin between Crystal's eyebrows relaxed into sleep, and then she studied the woman Zak had married. Had he loved her? Despite his denials, Jilly thought he must have cared for her at one time. Must still, according to her sisters, and Jilly feared they were right. After all, Crystal left Zak a long time ago, but he had never bothered to dissolve their marriage. Wasn't that proof that he still loved her?

The notion hurt too much to think about. One thing Jilly knew for certain, she couldn't let Zak know how she felt. He had enough to worry about without feeling guilty that his best friend was crazy in love with him.

Crystal slept on, the heavy rise and fall of her bird chest a sign that her pain had eased.

"Thank You, Lord," Jilly whispered. She rubbed the back of Crystal's hand and prayed quietly. For Crystal and her children. For Zak. For this awful, bewildering situation to somehow come out for the best.

At the end of her prayer, she felt no better. The heaviness of compassion and helplessness weighed her down.

How much worse must it be for Zak?

She should leave now, slip quietly out the door and go back to her dogs and her rabbits and her diabetic, nagging mother who meant well even though her words hurt like a sharp stick in the eye.

But she didn't. She couldn't. No matter what Mom thought. She was needed here.

After a while, the mess in Zak's home called to her and she set about to clean up. One of Zak's baseball socks peeked from beneath a chair. She dragged it out, carried it to his bedroom. The room was a man cave, a place where the real Zak lived. A flat screen on one wall, a computer and an iPod with a Bose sound system on the others, and all around reminders that Zak Ashford loved two earthly things: baseball and fighting fires. His poster of 9-11 firefighters surrounded by angels put a hitch in her throat.

She placed the sock on the end of his bed and stood breathing in the essence of the man she loved.

Mother wouldn't approve.

A clatter of voices broke the stillness.

Lungs filled with the faint scent of Zak's woodsy cologne and baseball leather, she made a hasty exit toward the living room.

"Jilly," Zak said. He looked tired, the lines around his eyes deeper today. An undeniable tenderness flared inside Jilly. A tender yearning to make things easier and better for him. The desire to hold him and be held, to snuggle on the couch and rub his tired shoulders.

"I thought you were still working, so I came over to make sure the kids had eaten. Crystal's asleep." Her voice sounded normal and calm, thank goodness, not giving away her random thoughts.

Zak scrubbed a hand over Jake's short hair. "Got these guys some equipment."

"I see that. Fancy." Jilly smiled at the oversized fielder's gloves, stiff and new, on each boy's hand and the tiny pink one on Bella's. "I guess I should go."

"Stick around. We'll play some ball."

"Yeah, Jilly, play with us," Jake said, dark eyes hopeful.

A wise woman would have sense enough to leave.

Jilly stayed.

Chapter Eight

He wanted to make Jilly laugh.

Zak lobbed the ball to Jake, whooping with pride when the boy stuck his new glove out and made contact. Granted, the ball dropped to the grass and Bella ran over to grab it, which started a game of tug-of-war. Brandon hopped in to protect Bella and then all three rolled around on the grass.

So Zak joined them.

In seconds, the kids were giggling, Zak was tickling and the trio dogpiled him. The boys held his arms down, a task they'd never have accomplished if he'd resisted, and Bella climbed aboard his chest.

He growled like a bear and pretended to struggle.

More giggles that did his heart good and snatched away his fatigue.

Bella patted one side of his face and honked his nose with her babyish fingers. Brandon laughed aloud. Zak stilled. He'd never heard Brandon laugh.

Emotion flooded his chest, a tide of pity and affection and something else he couldn't name.

Jilly loped over from her position on first base, hands on hips, and laughed down at the tangled mess of humanity.

He was glad Jilly lived next door. Just having her around

eased his stress, made life with the rug rats and Crystal easier. He'd seen the cleaning she'd done. He felt the care she gave to these pitiful little kids. And to him.

Yeah, to him. Jilly cared about him.

Fatigue was messing with his mind, making him sappy.

To stop the flow of unwanted thoughts and emotions, Zak snaked out a hand, snagged Jilly's ankle and yanked her down.

She tumbled forward with a yelp and a sputter, and then gales of laughter.

That thing in his chest welled up again.

His long arms and wide shoulders had broken Jilly's fall so she landed half on him, partly on the grass and partly on Brandon's legs. Her face crashed into his neck. For an infinitesimal moment, her breath fanned his skin. Ripples of pleasure caught him off guard.

Quickly, she pulled away, face inches from his chin. He tilted upward to meet her eye. She laughed again. Adorable freckles popped out against her milk-white skin. He loved her skin. She was pretty in a girl-next-door kind of way.

Nah, Jilly was pretty any old way. Without thinking, he did what came naturally, what he wanted to do, and stroked two fingers over her cheek.

Silk and heat to his calluses and leather.

His inner male hissed.

He moved his hand, forced a smile. "Your nose is sunburned."

Her hand went to the tip. She made a cute face.

In the brief lull, Jake saw his chance and threw himself atop Zak's chest, knocking Jilly sideways. Zak was both annoyed and relieved, considering the bizarre churning in his blood the moment he'd touched Jilly's skin.

The stress must be getting to him.

With a whoop, his suddenly intriguing neighbor popped up from the cool grass, put both boys in a headlock and gently thumped their heads together. Zak laughed. The pair sniggered.

"Didn't hurt."

"Oh, yeah?" Jilly challenged as she released them.

Zak sat up on the grass, knees bent, enjoying the interchange. Not to be left out, Bella jumped on his back and squeezed her small arms around his neck. Her slight weight was nothing compared to the people he'd carted out of burning buildings. She was a butterfly who smelled like grass and the taco he'd bought her for dinner.

"Ahoy, Zak Ashford. Jilly Fairmont."

GI Jack and Popbottle Jones stood at the edge of his house next to a blue bicycle. He'd never known them to ride a bike. Walk, yes. Occasionally drive an ancient, rebuilt truck, but not a bicycle. But nothing the pair did surprise anyone in Redemption. If they flew over in a homemade airplane, the town would take it in stride. They were, in a word, unique.

Even though the June weather heated the early evening, the aptly named Popbottle Jones, thanks to an overly long neck, wore a long-sleeved shirt with frayed cuffs and a pair of fingerless gloves. For his Dumpster-diving business, Zak assumed. And his baggy brown trousers and scuffed shoes, like most of his clothes, had seen better days.

GI Jack, the grizzled old soldier with the soft heart, wore a ratty camouflaged cap, gray hair sticking out from all sides. They were a fascinating pair of eccentrics, but they were much more, too. At least, to the people of Redemption.

"Popbottle. GI." Zak gave a welcoming wave and then rose with Bella clinging to his back like a small, blond, really cute monkey, and jogged toward the two old men. Bella belly laughed in his ear, a sweet gurgling sound. He had the fleeting wonder if any man had ever before given her a piggyback ride.

"Good evening, Zak Ashford," Popbottle Jones said in his formal professor's voice. "And this little miss," he said, tapping Bella's folded hands. "Bella, isn't it?"

"I twee," she declared, holding up two fingers and a thumb. "You got candy?"

"Bella," Zak protested with an embarrassed laugh. "Don't ask people for candy."

The old men chuckled, too.

"Quite all right," Popbottle said and reached into his shirt pocket for a peppermint—the kind given out at fast food restaurants.

Bella took it with a squeal of delight. "Candy!"

"She won't choke, will she?" GI fretted.

Too late, Bella had already popped the peppermint into her mouth. Considering he'd caught her eating rocks, Zak didn't worry much. "She'll be all right. Say thank you, Bella."

"Tank you. You gots candy for Jake and Bannon?"

Zak rolled his eyes, although the way the kids looked out for each other touched him.

By now the remaining ballplayers joined the conversation. Bella squirmed, so he let her slide slowly down his back to the ground.

The boys, he noticed, stared with interest at the bicycle.

GI Jack caught their gazes and asked, "Can either of you boys ride a bike?"

Brandon, who'd been hanging back, face tight at the appearance of strangers, stepped up. "I can. Jake's too little."

"Well, now, son, tell you what. I got this bicycle all fixed up and my old knees can't do a thing with it. A bike needs a boy. I was wondering if maybe you'd take it off my hands."

Brandon's eyes widened, his mouth dropped. His voice gushed out in a rush of disbelieving air. "You mean it?"

"Well, sure I do. On one condition. You teach your little brother how to ride, too."

Eagerly, the overly serious child nodded, his chest expanding in delight. Almost reverently, he advanced on the bicycle to touch the gleaming red fender. Zak thought the kid might explode. "I will. I promise."

"Well, now." GI Jack rubbed his chin. "What do you think, Popbottle? Is Brandon the right boy for this here bike?"

"That he is, GI." The old professor's wrinkled face spread in a smile. "A match made in heaven."

"A real bike." Brandon's words were a sigh. His brown eyes flashed toward Zak. "Can I ride it? Can I?"

"Go ahead. Stay in the driveway or on the grass."

"Come on, Jake, I'll show you how." Brandon straddled the bicycle and waddled it away from the adults. His brother and sister tagged alongside, chattering in excited tones.

"Really nice of you, GI Jack," Jilly said.

"Ah, it wasn't nothing. We had a bunch of old bike parts piled around. Even had a few cans of paint the hardware store tossed out."

A gifted junk artist with a knack for taking things other folks consider junk and making them new, GI Jack was known for his unexpected and absolutely perfect gifts.

Popbottle said, "It brings joy to my soul to hear a child's laughter."

GI's head bobbed. "Yep, joy to the soul."

Sure enough, the faint shouts and laughs circled around the house to bring smiles to the adults.

"Sweet children," Popbottle said.

Zak wanted to snort but refrained. Little did they know the rug rats were like three Tasmanian devils released in his house. The only thing that slowed them down was sleep.

"How is their mother?" GI removed his cap and fiddled with the brim. "We heard she wasn't faring well."

"She's not," Zak admitted, feeling guilty but not knowing why.

"Is the lady receiving visitors?"

Popbottle's question gave him pause. Church women had brought toys and a few casseroles. The nurse came daily. Jilly, too. But otherwise, he hadn't considered that Crystal needed company.

There came the guilt again.

"I'm not sure she's up to it," he said, turning to Jilly. His next-door neighbor was quiet. "What do you think?"

"Mostly, she sleeps. She's taking so much medication," Jilly said by way of explanation. "I sat with her awhile today, but we didn't talk much."

"Seeing the kids once or twice a day wears her out."

"I see. Then the prognosis is correct. Time is short."

Zak nodded. Even though he dealt with life-and-death issues on the job, he didn't like to talk about Crystal's death. He didn't like to think about it, either. Her death would free him in a way, and he was shamed to let the thought come.

He heard Jake's shout and Brandon's answering laugh. Responsibility bore down, and the fatigue of two days without sleep pulled at his body.

What was to become of Crystal's kids?

Popbottle took a small booklet from his pocket. "Long ago someone gave this to me. A dear friend now in Glory. Perhaps you would share this with the lady."

As he accepted the book, its red letters declaring, "The Way of Faith," shame flooded Zak. Everyone knew by now that the woman living in his house was dying. And that he was married to her. But never once had he shared his faith and his hope for eternity.

* * *

Jilly waved goodbye to the two old men as they rambled out of the yard and down the street, fading from sight with the waning sunset.

She was painfully aware of the man at her side. They'd had fun this evening, although Zak had to be so tired that he couldn't see straight. And that moment on the grass when he'd touched her cheek had felt more than neighborly.

"I should go," she said. "You need some sleep."

Zak snagged her wrist. "No. Stay. I'm not that tired."

She waffled, wanting to be with him and remembering her mother's words. Would the two Dumpster divers tell everyone she'd been with Zak, playing in the backyard while Zak's wife was inside the house dying?

"We should see where the kids are."

"I hear them. They're out front." He tugged at her arm. "Come on, keep me company. We'll sit in the lawn chairs and watch them fight over the bike."

In plain view of Jilly's house and her mother.

When she hesitated, he pressed, giving her his crooked Zak smile—the one that got her every time. "I could use a friend."

So could she. A friend who'd take her to get her head examined.

She caved. She always caved when it came to Zak. Mother was right. She was pathetic.

They made their way to the front yard and Zak's lawn chairs. He hadn't sat in one since Crystal moved in. He needed this, she realized. He needed time and relaxation. He needed her.

The corner streetlight quivered on, almost invisible against the last flames of sunset that shot red and pink and purple on the three children and their one bicycle.

Sweet Jake ran alongside his brother and Bella tried to

do the same, although with her short, chubby legs she fell quickly behind. Brandon pedaled slowly, the bike wobbling, to keep his siblings near.

There was good in that child for all his moodiness. She waved at him and called encouragement. He grinned.

Bless GI Jack, his talented hands and his wise, gentle heart.

"You want a Pepsi or something?" Zak asked. "I'm parched."

"I'll get it." She started to get up. "You're tired."

He pushed her back into the webbed chair. "You work, too."

Ah, Zak, she thought as he loped into the house, *see why I love you? See why you stole my heart? You're such a good guy.*

She'd turned to watch the children, enjoying their carefree moment, when she heard Zak's approach. Before she could swivel her head, he stuck a frosty can to the back of her neck.

She squealed and leaped up, knocking over her chair.

Zak laughed, mischievous eyes dancing. "Gotcha."

She whacked his shoulder. "I'll get you back."

"I know." He handed her a drink and collapsed into the chair beside her, long legs stretched out. "That's what makes it fun."

"Crystal okay?" she asked, settling again. She was certain he'd peeked in on his houseguest.

"Asleep or pretending to be. She seldom talks to me. Annie thinks she's depressed."

"Who could blame her?"

He aimed his soda at the kids. "Look at that."

Brandon held the bike while Jake climbed aboard.

"Any progress on finding a family?" she asked quietly.

He sipped his pop and stared into the encroaching twilight at the soon-to-be orphans. She did the same. "No. None. Pastor Parker's trying. I work with a guy whose wife is a social worker. She's got her ear to the ground. So does my lawyer."

"What's to become of them?"

The question agitated him. "I don't know, Jilly. They're not my kids. I wish people would believe that."

She touched her damp soda can to the hand he'd clamped on the chair arm. "I do."

His shoulders relaxed. "Sorry to vent. Not your fault. You've been great."

"Vent all you need. That's what friends are for." *But I don't want to be your friend. Not anymore.*

Oh, God, am I a bad person to think such a thing?

"Between this situation with Crystal and the rash of fires, I'm a little on edge."

"Just a little?" she teased.

"Yesterday's fire was arson," he said grimly. "It wasn't the first. With this drought, the dry grass and a town filled with hundred-fifty-year-old buildings…" He shook his head.

Jilly got the picture. "Any idea who might be responsible?"

"Not yet. The fire marshal suspects juveniles, bored with summer and nothing to do. That's usually the case."

"But it could be anyone with a bad attitude."

"Or someone who gets a buzz out of watching things burn and watching firefighters put themselves on the line."

"That's scary."

"Yeah." He chugged the last of his Pepsi, finishing with a satisfied "aah." His cell phone chirped once, an alarm easily mistaken for a cricket. Zak grinned and whipped out the fancy phone. "Game's on."

"Who's playing?" Not that the teams mattered. Zak watched them all if he could.

"Rockies and the Mets. De la Rosa's on the mound."

"Lefty," she said, to let him know she recognized the name. "Is he on your fantasy team?"

"Nope. Gotta get his ERA down."

"You could take his place."

He shot her that smile and squeezed her hand atop the metal chair arm. "Maybe."

"You could. You just need the scouts to see you pitch. You looked amazing out there yesterday." In more ways than one.

"I need more time to work out and get the arm in top shape. Right now, time is hard to find. Once the fire danger subsides I'll work out at the station. Staying in shape is part of the job, you know."

She did. Zak had told her about the weight room at his station and the importance of a firefighter staying in top shape. Someone's life, even his own, could depend on his physical conditioning. To her, he looked in awesome shape. "From what I've seen, you've never pitched better."

He rotated his arm. "I'm throwing pretty well. The fast ball's there. My change-up's improved. If I can make the All-Star Squad..."

A child's pained cry broke into the conversation. Both adults bolted upright.

"Jakey!" Bella screamed.

Jilly squinted into the gathering darkness. "Jake's wrecked."

"He'll be okay. Kids wreck." But Zak rushed toward the fallen child lying at the bottom of the driveway just the same.

Brandon was already struggling to get the downed bike off his brother. The action brought louder cries from Jake.

"My foot. Stop!"

Brandon backed away, lips tight and eyes frightened, his stance small and defensive.

Zak went to one knee beside the bicycle. Jilly did the same on the other side. She grimaced at the sight. Somehow Jake's foot had slid sideways in between the wheel spokes and was trapped. Each time he tried to move his foot, pressure from the wires made him cry out.

Zak smoothed Jake's sweaty hair and spoke softly. "Easy, Jake. We'll have you out of there in a minute."

Zak's first responder hands slid gently over the boy's lower leg and down to the trapped ankle. He was testing, she thought, for a break. When he inserted his fingers between the wire and skin, Jake cried out.

"Jakey, Jakey!" Bella screamed.

"Hush, Bella." Jilly drew the distraught toddler to her side. "He'll be okay."

"Will you have to cut his leg off?" Brandon's question brought another round of cries and groans from the fallen boy. "Is he gonna die?"

"Stop, all of you. Listen to me." Jilly spoke firmly as she put a hand on Brandon's back. He trembled, but for once he didn't shy away. "He's not going to die and no one will cut his leg off. Zak will take care of him."

"Of course I will," Zak said, his calm, confident manner flowing into the scared kids. Dusk was upon them and seeing the wires wasn't easy. "Brandon, get the flashlight from my truck. Remember where it is under the seat?"

Brandon darted off and returned in less than a minute with the light.

"Shine it right there where Jake's foot is. See?" He directed the shaking boy, giving him a part in rescuing his brother.

Zak's pitching-strong fingers gripped the spokes and

slowly stretched them apart. "Jilly, see if you can ease his foot out."

Jilly did as he directed and in seconds Jake's foot slipped clear. Instantly, Zak swooped the boy into his arms and with long-limbed strides headed for the house. Everyone followed.

"You're okay now, buddy," he was saying as he lowered Jake to the couch and removed his sneaker. "Let me have a look."

Brandon rushed to his brother's side, staring down with trembling lip. "His leg is broke."

Jilly put a hand on his shoulder and shook her head at him. "Don't say that."

The poor kid always took the pessimistic view.

Zak ran expert fingers over the red indentations on Jake's ankle and foot. Jake sniffled and sucked his thumb but didn't cry out.

"Should we take him to the E.R.?" Jilly asked, hovering.

"I don't think anything is broken, but we'll ice it down for a while and reassess."

"Can I go to the bathroom first?" Jake asked.

"Need help?"

Brandon shouldered in. "He can lean on me."

Zak and Jilly exchanged glances. Brandon needed to do this. The two adults stepped back and watched as little brother leaned on big brother. Jake hopped on one foot sniffing, with serious-faced Brandon guiding. By the time they returned, Jake had tired of hopping and reentered the living room walking with only a slight limp.

"I'm all well," he said. "Can I ride the bike tomorrow? I won't get hurt. I promise."

Zak breathed out a loud sigh of relief. "Tonight, ice." He lofted a cold pack. "Tomorrow, we'll see. Prop your foot up on these pillows Jilly fixed. Brandon, time for baths and bed."

Brandon rolled his eyes but herded Bella toward the bathroom. Jilly felt for the kid. He seemed convinced his siblings were his responsibility.

"I'll bathe Bella," she said. "You take care of you."

Zak gave her a tired glance. "Thanks. I should look in on Crystal."

By the time the kids were bathed and had said their good-nights to a lethargic Crystal, Jilly's shoulders ached and the events of the day pressed in. She didn't know how Zak held up under the strain. Mom could criticize all she wanted, but Zak needed her.

Carrying a droopy Bella who smelled like Zak's manly soap in her plastic pull-up and clean cotton nightgown, Jilly entered the bedroom shared by the siblings. Even though she had no idea where he'd gotten them, Zak had installed a set of bunk beds and a toddler bed. This room had housed his exercise and pitching equipment before.

"Prayer time." Zak clapped his hands once. "Take a knee."

Jilly couldn't help smiling. Zak was such a baseball player. She'd heard him say the same thing to teammates before a ball game.

The trio lined up alongside the bottom bunk, elbows on the blanket and hands folded. From the back, they were a picture of perfection, a Norman Rockwell painting of child-hood innocence and faith. She wanted to hug them all, to gather them up and spare them from the tragedy no one could stop.

Zak hitched a chin toward Jilly, motioning for her to follow as he joined the kids on his knees. Jilly's chest filled with emotion. A big, manly man with such a godly heart.

The kids prayed, something she felt sure Zak had taught

them. She peaked at the three little ones and at him, heads bowed and intent on talking to God. They took turns giving thanks. For the bike, the new baseball gloves and that Jake's foot wasn't broken.

When Jake murmured, "Make Mama feel better," anguish tightened Zak's face, and a thick lump filled Jilly's throat. He opened his eyes, caught her watching and shook his head in a gesture of helplessness.

There were some prayers God didn't answer.

Chapter Nine

"What am I going to do?" Zak asked, his voice quiet in the darkness of his front yard.

The rug rats were in bed, hopefully asleep, and Jilly was about to head across the street to her own bed.

Tired as he was, he didn't want her to leave. He stalled, stuck his hands in his pants' pockets, and looked up at the inky, speckled sky.

"You're doing the best you can." Her voice was hushed, too, as though afraid of waking the children. She couldn't know they slept like the dead.

He winced. Poor choice of words, considering.

"I'll go," she said. "You're exhausted."

"Yeah." He grasped her elbow, winced again at the slight pain in his hands, and released her. "Thanks."

"I saw your hand."

"No big deal."

"Can you pitch?"

"It'll heal fast. Just a wire cut."

She shifted, took his hand and held it toward the light coming from the front window. "Put something on it."

"Yes, Doc."

She smiled and started to release him. He closed his fingers around hers. She looked up, questioning.

"You're the best friend I've ever had." He didn't know why he was spilling his guts. Fatigue, he supposed. Maudlin, like a drunk, although he was drunk on lack of sleep.

"And don't you forget it," she tried to joke, but there was a catch in her voice. He heard it, wondered about it.

He tugged on her hand, pulled her to his side and dropped an arm over her shoulder. She felt right against him.

The night was warm with honeysuckle playing tag with the wind and the distant sounds of eighteen-wheelers up on the main highway.

"Look," he said, pointing.

Fireflies, like a net of tiny white Christmas lights, enveloped a bush near the door. Butterfly weed, Jilly called the flowers and she came over every spring to poke at the base with a little spade and extract the yearly promise that he wouldn't cut it down. He'd promised, but he'd been tempted. Bushes and flowers were easy prey for a man with a weed whacker.

"When I was a kid, my brother and I would chase them until Mom called us in."

"Me, too. We put them in an old mayo jar and watched them glow. I love fireflies. Such beautiful little creatures." She sighed, moving her head just a little so that her face tilted up toward him, shadowed in the palest light. "Mom would also say to let them go, but I'd forget."

"And the next morning, they'd be dead." He remembered the disappointment, the remorse that he'd caused their deaths by trapping them.

"Yes, but there were always more the next night."

His lips curved. Jilly, the animal lover, the vet assistant.

"Wanna chase some?"

"Not tonight." She shook her head, face still tilted up toward his. "Love bugs."

His heart stuttered. "What?"

"We called them love bugs." Her voice smiled. "They're mating, you know."

"Oh, right." He didn't feel like smiling. Jilly's nearness and her talk of love bugs shorted out his brain. He had the strongest urge to bend just a little and kiss her. The darkness covered them. No one would see.

Love bugs.

"Jilly?" he said, surprised when her name was a whisper.

Her expression shifted and something in her eyes answered the question in his voice. "Zak?"

In a fluid, athletic move, he turned her into his arms and held her lightly. His heart hammered against his ribs in both fear and thrill. This was Jilly, his next-door neighbor, his best friend.

And he wanted to kiss her more than anything he could think of.

He was going to kiss her.

The butterflies in Jilly's stomach quivered with anticipation. Zak was going to kiss her. Finally, at last, she was in his arms where she'd dreamed of being.

And she couldn't let it happen.

Yearning warred with common sense, and the woman who rescued rabbits and took care of her mother's diabetes gave into common sense.

Regretfully, she placed a palm against Zak's chest to push him away. Just as regretfully, she felt the rise and fall of his breathing, the staccato rhythm of his heart beneath his fireman's T-shirt, and remembered he was not hers.

"I have to go," she said in a shaky whisper.

He released her immediately and stepped back, another cause for regret. In a low voice, he said, "Thanks for everything."

"Anytime. That's what neighbors are for." The words sounded false to her ears. Love thy neighbor didn't mean like this.

She started to turn away, but Zak caught her hand. "See you tomorrow?"

"Sure." Pretend that nothing had happened, that he hadn't almost kissed her.

Then she walked away, crossed the silent street and the soft cushion of her front lawn. Everything in her wanted to turn back, to step into his arms again and see what would have happened.

At her front door, she paused with one hand on the knob, uncomfortably cognizant of the lamplight from the front room. Mom was still up. One glance at Jilly's face and she would know something had happened, for surely the accursed blush was high on her cheeks and her freckles stood at attention.

As if drawn by a giant magnet, she turned her head and glanced across the street to where a tall, lanky firefighter remained shadowed in the night. Her heart leaped a little to know he was still there, watching, maybe thinking about her.

He raised a hand. She responded in kind, wishing for what could not be, for what she could not allow and still face herself and her God in the light of day.

"Why now, Lord?" she whispered into the darkness. She'd waited so long for this to happen, for Zak to notice her as a woman. "Why now?"

"Looking a little grim, Ash. Problems?" Zak's supervisor, Captain Ron Porter, clapped him on the shoulder.

They'd just come in from an MVA out on a county road. A local teenager going too fast on a gravel surface failed to negotiate a turn and flipped his truck. The teen was okay. The truck wasn't. The routine call was not the cause of Zak's problems.

"I'm okay."

"Good job out there today during victim extraction. The kid was shook. Talking baseball calmed him."

Zak shrugged. All he had done was his job and a little talking. The noise and violent ripping of the Jaws of Life could make anyone antsy.

"I spotted a ball and glove on the floorboard. Figured talking baseball would distract him."

"That's what makes you good at your job. Keen observation. Like mine. So what's eating at you? The home situation?"

Zak sighed. All the guys knew but over the days, the teasing had turned to silent sympathy. No one said much, probably because like him, they didn't know what to say. "Yeah."

More than the home situation was eating a hole in him today. Last night with Jilly, in the yard, her in his arms... He couldn't get the image or the feelings out of his head. He'd been tempted to do something crazy, and this sudden awareness of his neighbor stunned him. When had Jilly become a fascinating female?

Then Jakey had suffered a nightmare and Bella had wet the bed. All the racket had awakened Crystal and she'd been in frightening pain. He'd given her the pain medication and sat beside her in a chair and did the only thing he could. He'd prayed and talked to her about heaven. After an hour, when the medication hadn't touched her, he'd called in the hospice nurse who was still there when he'd left for work this morning.

He tossed his helmet on the locker shelf and shrugged out of his gear.

"Cancer's a mean disease." He hated it, hated the helpless feelings, hated the pain Crystal suffered and hated the fear he saw on three kids' faces.

Captain Porter squeezed his shoulder in a show of quiet support.

The other firefighters moved around the open engine bay, cleaning and storing gear, setting up for the next run.

For a couple of years now, he'd worked with the captain, a forty-something firefighter with a quickly receding hairline that lengthened an already-long nose. Porter was a good leader, sensible, strong and supportive. Like the other guys, Captain didn't pry unless job performance was hindered.

"Am I slacking?" Zak asked.

Captain's lower lip protruded, pondering. "Maybe distracted."

Zak gave a bark of mirthless laughter. "I am that. Sorry, Captain. I'll do better."

"You're a top-notch firefighter, Zak. If you need some time off…"

"Thank you, sir. I'm fine." *Why is this happening, Lord?* Nothing made sense anymore.

The captain gazed at him steadily for a few seconds before walking away.

Zak banged his forehead against the wire shelf. When had his life gotten so completely out of control?

Firefighting and baseball were his passions. Yet, lately, his brain was anywhere but on the job or the baseball field. And the prayers he sent up seemed to hit the clouds and bounce back. Pastor Parker had offered council, but there was only so much gut spilling a man could do and still feel like a man. Besides, he didn't want the pastor knowing how resistant he was to taking care of his lawful wife. And her kids.

Worse, he felt uncomfortable in his own house, the one he'd committed to paying for over the next twenty-five years of his life. His man cave had become a combined hospital and play school and he tiptoed around in fear of disturbing Crystal. If he stepped on one more Friendly Meal toy in the middle of the night while rushing to the kids' room to see why Bella or Jakey was crying, he might be tempted to swear. Loudly.

His only peace had been here at the station or on the ball field, and he was doubly thankful for twenty-four-hour, sleep-at-the-station shifts. Except then he worried about the kids, about Crystal, about what had happened to his life.

And now his captain said he was distracted on the job.

Go figure.

He went into the common area set up like a living room with five recliners, a big TV and a kitchen area to one end. He flopped into a recliner and pointed the remote at ESPN. Other firefighters filtered in, talking about the run. Zak didn't feel up to idle chatter.

Last night's scores rolled across the bottom of the screen. De la Rosa had pitched a winning game.

Jilly said he could take de la Rosa's place. If given the chance, maybe he could.

Jilly's encouragement meant a lot. He couldn't get along without Jilly.

Was she upset with him today? Had she felt the same thing he had last night, whatever it had been?

He wanted to call her and explain. But explain what? That he'd wanted to kiss her? Or that he thought he might be caving to the stress and he'd been momentarily delusional? That he might be falling in love with her?

His stomach jumped into his throat. No way. Jilly was

his best friend. She could spit a sunflower seed farther than he could. Her batting swing was first rate, and she kept track of his ERA, his strikeouts, his walks. Jilly was his pal. She was…awesome and beautiful and self-sacrificing.

With a groan, he removed his cell phone and scanned to Jilly's number. She'd be at work this time of morning, having doughnuts from the Sugar Shack with the good doc and Jeri Burdine. He started to press the send key but paused. Didn't the clinic do animal surgery on Tuesday mornings?

Instead, he keyed a short text, erased it, pondered over what to say and finally gave up. What was wrong with him? He'd never had a problem talking to Jilly before.

He scrolled to the number of the hospice nurse, Annie Hawkins, who was both friend and medical professional. Better to touch base there, considering last night's issues, even though he had confidence in Annie's care of Crystal. She and Jilly were good friends, too. They even did the girly shopping thing together, something he avoided the way he avoided brussels sprouts.

"Hello." Annie's smooth professional tone came over the air waves.

"Annie, Zak. How's everything?"

"I was about to call you." She didn't sound happy.

Zak braced himself for bad news. "Is she still in pain?"

"Crystal is resting now, but she's very weak, Zak, and the pain is worsening." She paused, and he could envision her frown. Annie was a gentle, sympathetic woman. "I started her on a pump today, rather than pills."

"She needs the fluids."

"And the pain meds. There's no way to know for sure, but—"

"I understand." As a paramedic, he knew the signs of

fading life. Crystal might live days or weeks, but her body was giving up. "Are the kids okay? We had a rough night."

"Jilly's mom took Bella and Jake across the street for a while so Crystal could rest. They seemed relieved to get out of the house."

"Understandable." He felt the same.

"Yes, I thought so, too. Bless Diane for taking them. I saw them in the backyard playing with Jilly's rabbits. Brandon's riding his bike somewhere. I think they're okay, all things considered."

Kids and bunnies and Brandon on his bike cheered Zak a little. "Call me if you need me."

"Will do. Try not to worry."

Easy for her to say. "Thanks, Annie."

He tapped the screen to end the call and then held the phone against his chin, thinking. Time was running out. Both for Crystal and her kids.

He needed to talk to Jilly again, get her take, because ultimately, no matter how he bemoaned the task, he felt responsible for Crystal's children. Unless a family stepped forward—

The fire alarm sounded, piercing the station with an ear-splitting wail. The address came over the intercom. Another grass fire. Zak was up and out in the engine bay, geared up and ready before anyone else, determined not to let his captain down again. The fact that he'd rather fight a fire than deal with the troubling question of Crystal's children and their future didn't escape him. He'd never been a coward before, but he was scared out of his mind about this.

Chapter Ten

Citizens assumed grass fires weren't all that dangerous. They were wrong. A shift in wind direction, an unexpected brush flare and a firefighters could be trapped with no escape but death.

Today was all right so far, if incredibly hot, the air reeking of ash and cinder. Zak worked a whip line to knock down the tall prairie grass blaze in front of him with Trey Matthews on a high-pressure hose mopping up the hot spots.

The brush pumper tank was running low on water with the nearest hydrant a mile away. With a chuckle Zak wished they could recycle sweat. The stuff rolled off him in sheets.

Trey jostled up beside him, gear clanking, sweat-sheened, too. "Ash, Captain says fall back, let it go. We'll catch it at the road south. Unit two is coming to assist."

Zak scanned the horizon, aware his captain had already done the same, making sure no structure was in peril. The thick clouds of gray-and-black smoke obscured his vision and clogged his nostrils. In the near distance, he heard the wail of unit two en route. "Got it."

Dragging the heavy line and glad for the protective gear even if it was hot, Zak worked his way toward the fire truck parked on the north road. From the corner of his helmet, he glimpsed something shiny in the charred grass. After replacing the now-empty hose onto the back of the truck, he returned to the spot, curious.

Gear weighty against his body, he removed one glove and went down on his haunches to retrieve the small, silver object. The yellow toes of his boots were black with soot.

"What ya got there, Ash?"

Zak held the smoke-covered object out for Trey to see. "Spaceman. Wonder how it got here."

Trey shrugged. "Kids' meal toys are everywhere. My kid has a dozen."

"Yeah, I guess you're right." Zak pushed to a stand, still holding the toy. Every kid who bought a Friendly Meal received a free Spaceman or one of his buddies. They were a common item. Brandon and Jake had gotten one in last night's dinner. He bounced the toy in his hand a couple of times, bothered by a formless gut feeling, then pocketed the silver man and jogged to the truck for the ride around the section.

Zak didn't think about Spaceman again for several days. He simply didn't have the time. Besides work and worrying about Crystal and her crew, Jilly had disappeared on him. He'd texted her a couple of times and she'd responded, but she didn't come over. She'd missed his game, too. Jilly never missed a game!

Clearly, she'd been offended the other night when she'd spoken of love bugs and he'd almost kissed her.

Since then, he'd pitched twice, once as a starter and the other in middle relief when Taylor fell apart on the mound and the Lonewolf team was using the starter for easy batting practice. Redemption had lost, but Zak had pitched well, his ERA coming down nicely. He'd even rated an interview for some sports guy's blog out of Dallas. Pretty sweet. Jilly's response to his jubilant text was a bland "Congrats."

Just for kicks, he'd looked himself up on the internet and watched a short clip on YouTube. Good thing, too. Coach hadn't said a word about the glitch Zak discovered in his windup.

He rotated his left shoulder, took his stance and went through the motions, paying careful attention to the minor twist of his foot during the movement. Gotta fix that. He'd get Jilly to film his next game for study.

He stopped. His shoulders dropped. Jilly. Man, he missed her. Maybe later—

"Zak." Small voices around his house still caught him off guard.

He glanced down at the big brown eyes. The kid would be cute if he'd keep his thumb out of his face and lose the worry frown. "What's up, Jakey?"

"Can we play catch?" The boy cast an anxious glance at the baseball in Zak's hand. Poor kid hadn't figured out Zak carried a ball everywhere except in his fire gear.

"Sure, dude. Grab a glove. Brandon, too, if he wants."

"He's gone."

Zak frowned. Gone meant one thing. Brandon was riding his bike. The problem with that was the kid never told anyone where he went. He just rode off.

"Let me look in on your mom," Zak said, following Jake down the hall toward the bedrooms. The floor needed vacuuming. Again. He sighed. He couldn't afford a housekeeper, but man, the place got messy fast.

He eased open the door to Crystal's room, watched the rise and fall of her labored breathing before quietly closing the door again.

"Asleep," he whispered to Jakey's upturned face.

Jake gnawed a bottom lip. "I read her a story."

"Nice deal. I'm sure she liked that."

The boy's thumb edged toward his mouth. "She fell asleep."

Zak touched the anxious child, deflecting the encroaching thumb. "That's a good thing, Jakey. It means you made her feel better."

"I did?" Halfway to the mouth, the thumb faltered and dropped.

"Sure, you did."

"She sleeps a lot. I wish she could wake up. I miss her."

A sad sigh welled in Zak's chest. He gripped the little boy's damp hand. *Help me out here, God.* "She's very sick."

"I don't want her to die." Tears welled in Jake's eyes.

"Listen, Jakey boy, I know this is hard for you to understand." It was hard for him to understand, too. "Hang in there, okay?"

Such a feeble thing to say and no comfort, he was sure. But Jakey nodded solemnly and clutched the baseball glove against his scrawny chest with both hands. The obvious attempt not to suck his thumb got to Zak.

They made their way outside to the modest backyard, now strewn with kids' toys and his baseball paraphernalia. Bella, who'd been watching cartoons, tagged along, jabbering about Max and Ruby, the cartoon bunnies. The grass had grown tall enough to brush the back of her bare, dimpled knees. One more thing to add to his to-do list. Mow the grass before one of the little ones disappeared completely. Mowing grass made him think of Jilly and her cranky old mower and the way she looked in white shorts with her red hair shining like a new penny beneath the summer sun.

He gently tossed the ball to Jake. When the boy missed as usual, Zak held his glove up, showing the correct form. "Like this, Jake. Not this."

When Jake didn't get it the first time, Zak jogged over, demonstrated and tried again.

Meanwhile, Bella found a plastic shovel and deepened the hole the kids had dug under the big shady elm. A man could break a leg in that canyon, but he didn't have the heart to complain. These kids were hurting enough.

Standing only a few feet away from his playmate, he continued to toss the ball with Jake, cheering and teaching. Watching the boy go from perpetual frown to a proud grin made him feel good. He'd always liked coaching Little League, a position he'd forsaken this summer.

"Bella," he yelled, spotting her from the corner of his eye. "Don't eat the rock. Spit it out."

To his amazement, the blond charmer did exactly that, smiled and batted big eyes. She was going to be a man magnet like her mom.

The thought stuck in his chest. Crystal's magnetic force had drawn all the wrong kind of men. By her own admittance, she'd made bad choices. Lots of them. He didn't want that to happen to Bella. Or Jake. Or Brandon.

About that time, Brandon rode into the yard on the shiny bike. Zak turned in his direction just as Jake let loose of a fast ball. The pitch caught Zak on the side of the head.

He stumbled back, stunned, and barely had time to register the dull throb of pain when Jake slammed into his legs.

"Zak! Don't die. I'm sorry." The howler set sail, ripping the peaceful neighborhood with his fear and remorse. Zak went to his haunches and wrapped the thin body in a bear hug. The warm essence of sweaty kid swamped him with unexpected tenderness.

"I'm okay, buddy. You didn't hurt me."

The howler ceased. With a sniff, he said, "I didn't mean to hit you. I'm sorry."

Zak tilted his head to display the spot near his temple. "Is it red?"

"Yes."

"Swollen?"

Jake's shoulders bunched. Hiccuping, he shuddered, ready to cry at the drop of a hat. "I don't know."

"No." Brandon had parked his bike and come over to inspect Zak's wound. "It's not puffy at all."

"There ya go, then, sport. I'm not hurt. Okay?" He patted Jake's chest. "You can't hurt a firefighter. We're tough."

Apparently mollified, Jake stayed snuggled against him, the same sweet way he and Bella did every night when Zak was home to watch TV or tuck them in. Brandon was the hard case, hanging back. Zak realized then that they were growing on him. Resist all he would, he was starting to care about the rug rats.

He reached out and tugged Brandon toward him. Stiffly, the nine-year-old came closer until his shoulder touched Zak's.

"Where you been, bud?" Zak asked.

Face bland, Brandon answered, "Nowhere."

That's what he always said.

Zak untangled himself from Jake and stood, a hand on each boy's shoulder. "Wanna play catch?"

Brandon shrugged. "I guess so."

Such enthusiasm.

A siren tore through the air. Out of habit, Zak rotated toward the sound, attentive. Beneath Zak's grip, Brandon tensed.

"Gotta get my glove." He slithered away from Zak's touch. "It's only a grass fire."

Zak turned a thoughtful look on the bike rider. "What makes you think that?"

"I don't know." Then he took off, running for the back door as if someone was chasing him.

Zak picked up the baseball and rubbed his fingers over the rough stitching. The feel of the round, stitched leather soothed him. He thought of the last fire he'd fought and the Spaceman he'd found at the site.

"Jake," he said. "Didn't you and Brandon get a Spaceman in your Friendly Meals?"

"Yes. You wanna play Spaceman? We just gots one. Brandon lost his."

Zak shook his head, the nagging worry like acid in his gut. He needed to talk to Jilly. She'd tell him he was all wet. He hoped.

Jilly's belly jumped as wildly as the terriers leaping around Zak's sneakered feet.

"Hi."

He stood at her front door, looking really, really good in a baseball pullover and cargo shorts. She'd missed him.

"You been avoiding me?"

Yes. "Don't be silly. Come in. Mama made brownies."

Once upon a time, he would have said, "I'm gonna have to marry that woman." But not anymore. Not since Crystal.

The reason she'd been avoiding him crowded in like bad breath in an elevator.

"Brownies sound amazing. Got milk?"

She smiled a little and let him in, thinking of how perfect he would be in those milk commercials with a baseball in one hand and a milk glass in the other. All lanky six-feet-something of him ducked under the ceiling fan as he sauntered toward the kitchen. She loved the loose-limbed easy way he moved as if he had all the time in the world. The illusion was deceiving given how fast he could move on the playing field.

"You missed my games."

"Sorry." She'd purposely made other plans, including a makeup dinner with her sister who'd grabbed the occasion to set Jilly up with a guy from her office. Mel was a nice-enough guy, but all Jilly could think was that her heart was already taken.

Zak slouched into a kitchen chair and stuck his long legs out. She stepped over them to the counter, the smell of rich chocolate rising from the warm brownie pan with the power of a siren's song.

"Make yourself at home," she said, a little testily, remembering Nicole's doormat comment. "Let me serve you."

Her tone surprised him. She could tell because he gathered all that long length and stood. "I'll get the milk."

He poured a tall glass, hitched the carton and an eyebrow to ask if she wanted some, too.

"Half a glass. I'm on a diet."

He groaned. "Not again. You look good to me."

"Right." If she looked all that great, why hadn't he noticed at some point during the past five years? Feeling out of sorts, she plopped a brownie on a napkin in front of him. "Here."

"Are you mad at me?"

"Don't be silly."

"Meaning yes." He propped an elbow on the table, forsaking his brownie momentarily. "Whatever I did, I'm sorry."

"You would be." *Let it go, Jilly.*

With a bewildered frown, he shoved half a fudgy brownie in his mouth and chewed. "Are you okay?"

"Sure." *My heart hurts and I want to leap on your lap and kiss your face off, but you're married. So yes, I'm just dandy.*

"Good. I'm glad. I thought maybe..." He sipped the milk, backhanding the inevitable and utterly appealing milk mustache.

Men could be so clueless.

Which was a good thing, she supposed. If he had already forgotten that amazing, tempting moment in his front yard, she should be glad.

Then why wasn't she?

"I need to talk to you about something important," Zak was saying.

Jilly's pulse ratcheted up. Apparently, he hadn't forgotten, even though he must. They could not go there. Not now. She didn't want to discuss the near kiss, the feelings that had simmered between them. She popped a fat bite of brownie onto her tongue. Nothing like rich chocolate, sweet and fattening to resolve stress. Forget the diet.

"It's Brandon."

She gulped down a cakey lump.

"Brandon?" *Not the kiss we didn't share. The one I've imagined so many times I'm embarrassed to face you?*

Had she imagined the entire episode?

Zak's milk glass clinked softly against the tabletop. He circled it, leaving damp spots on the glass top.

"I'm hoping you'll tell me I'm off base, but I suspect he has something to do with the recent grass fires."

"Brandon?" she said again, stupidly. "Why would you think that?"

"Remember the day he wandered away from the ball game?" He waited for her nod. "He never said where he'd been, but we heard the fire truck minutes after we found him."

"Coincidence."

"It's happened twice more, and just now he rode up on his bike from 'nowhere' again."

Jilly put a hand to her lips. "I heard the siren."

"Yeah." He rubbed a hand over his eyes, weariness and worry taking a toll. And Jilly, being Jilly, wanted to rush in and make things better for him. *Doormat.*

"The weird thing is," he went on, "Brandon heard it, too, and said it was a grass fire. Why would he say such a thing unless he knew?"

"Have you called the station to verify?"

"Yes." Face grim, he nodded. "It's grass."

"Oh, Zak. Surely, this is all coincidence."

"I want to think so, but I found this at one of the burn sites." He took a small silver figure from his pocket. "Spaceman. Brandon can't find his. I asked."

"But that doesn't mean *this* particular Spaceman is his. Lots of kids have them."

"No, but it looks bad. And I have this gnawing in my gut." The corner of his lip tilted. "And it's not from eating Diane's brownies."

Jilly returned the smile. "A missing trinket doesn't make him guilty."

"What if I'm right?" His Converse sneakers scraped restlessly on the brown tile. "I think I'm right, Jilly." He got up from the table to pace to the counter and back. "Call it fireman's instinct, but if he's not guilty, he's involved."

"He's only nine."

"Firebugs start young. With the emotional garbage he's going through, probably gone through, he may be releasing his anger and frustration in the only way he can."

"That kind of thing makes no sense to me."

"Lots of psychological behavior is senseless."

"True." She worried the condensation on her milk glass. "What should we do?"

Zak slouched back into his chair and squeezed the top

of her hand. One quick squeeze and release but enough to make her yearn for more. She was such a pushover.

"I like the way you said 'we.'"

Jilly tried to ignore the import of that one little word but couldn't. Dumb as it was, she thought of herself and Zak as a unit.

"Crystal's too sick to deal with this," she said. "We can't involve her."

"Agreed. We can't involve the police, either," he said, the ethical struggle clear on his face. "Brandon's not a criminal. He's a hurting kid."

"If he did this, Zak—" she held up a hand "—I still say you have no real evidence. But let's say he did. If we turn him over to Jesse Rainmaker, Crystal will have to know." The police chief was good-hearted, but he was also a fair and honest officer of the law.

"I'm not telling anyone but you at this point. Not until I'm sure." Restless as a housefly, he went to the counter for another brownie. "I'll keep a closer watch on him."

"How? When?" With his work schedule and a series of ball games coming up, how could he possibly do more?

Zak shoved a three-inch brownie in his mouth and said in a muffled, resigned tone, "I don't know."

Jilly handed him a napkin. "Chew and swallow, firedog."

He laughed, sputtering to hold in the brownie. Jilly laughed, too. It felt good and natural to laugh with Zak again over something as silly as a mouthful of brownie.

Zak must have felt the same because he hooked one sinewy arm around her neck in a buddy hug. "You're the best."

Yeah, yeah, I know. I'm the best. The best friend. The best neighbor. The best babysitter.

I'm a total loser.

The touch of his skin against hers stirred the memory

of the non-kiss. Aching inside, she turned aside, breaking contact to discard paper napkins. Brownie crumbs scattered on the floor. She went to one knee and bumped heads with Zak who'd apparently had the same compunction to keep Mom's floor clean.

"I'll get them."

Zak shouldered her. "Out of the way, civilian."

Mugsy raced in from another room, nose popping and tags jingling in wild excitement. The dog beat them both to the spray of crumbs. Jilly chuckled. "Why didn't I call him in the first place?"

Mugsy put his paws on Zak's knees, head cocked, black button eyes intense, stubby tail wagging madly.

"Sorry, Mugsy, I'm clean." Zak held out a hand for the dog's inspection. Mugsy swiped him with a pink tongue.

Jilly took the opportunity to move away.

He snagged her wrist. "Hey."

She froze, turned slightly but still on one knee, ready to rise. Her traitorous pulse stuttered. "What?"

"Your Mom's not here, right?"

"Weight Watchers."

His mouth—that wide, mobile, fascinating mouth— tilted up. "She made brownies."

"And ate three. That's why she went to Weight Watchers."

He nodded sagely. "Irrationally sensible."

"That's Mom." Jilly glanced down at his long, powerful fingers still manacling her narrow wrist. She'd never been delicate, but when compared with Zak's strength, she felt that way—feminine and small.

With his paramedic training, he could probably feel the rattle in her pulse. But it wasn't medical help Jilly needed. She needed to have her head examined. A lobotomy, maybe, to extricate Zak Ashford from her brain forever.

"About the other night," he started.

"What night?"

Heat crept up her neck and spread across her cheeks. She should have known playing clueless wouldn't work.

"Don't, Jilly. I can't stop thinking about it." He loosened his hold, but before she could move away, his fingers found hers, entwined and tugged. On her haunches, she unbalanced and tilted toward him, landing against his rock-hard thigh. Like a catcher taking on a slider at home plate, he never budged.

"You're my best friend," she squeaked. "What's to talk about?"

She pushed against his side and shoulder and tried to stand. He let her go and followed her up, green eyes searching hers. He was quiet for interminable seconds while Mugsy's toenails danced on the tile and Satchmo wandered in to check out the commotion.

"Do you ever wonder—" he crossed his arms, hands folded beneath his armpits in a familiar pitcher stance "—about you and me?"

Not now, Zak. Don't go there.

He did.

"If we might be more than friends. There's something going on here, at least for me."

Tension tightened a noose around her neck. "We can't."

His hands dropped to his sides and he stepped closer. "Can't? I don't get it."

"And I don't want to discuss this."

Gently, Zak gripped her upper arms with those long, wonderful hands. "We talk about everything. Always have. It's one of the things I…" His voice trailed off and he looked as bewildered as she was scared. "Don't freak out, but…I think I might be in love with you."

If he'd struck her with lightning, she wouldn't have been

more shocked and unprepared. As it was, she sucked in a joyful, "Oh," and reached one hand toward him. The reaction came unbidden from the deep place where she'd kept her love for so long and she could no more stop the reaction than she could destroy the love.

In that tiny window of opportunity when she was most vulnerable, Zak swooped in and pulled her close, green eyes searching hers. She went into his arms, too stunned to resist, and if truth was told, she didn't want to stop what was about to happen.

"Jilly," he said softly and then his lips touched hers.

Beautiful sensation washed through her. Sweet as brownie, warm as summer and soft as a butterfly wing. This was Zak, her love, the dream she'd held close for five years and now held close in reality. They'd touched before as friends, but this was different. His lanky, athletic body held her in an embrace as a man holds a woman he cherishes. Cherished. What a lovely word. What a lovely feeling. Had she ever felt cherished before? With heart hammering and pleasure rippling through every cell, she wanted the kiss and the moment to last forever, to wash away all the reasons kissing Zak was wrong and shouldn't happen.

And there it was like a flashing neon sign. This should not happen. Zak had a wife. Jilly was the other woman.

Shame replaced the joy. Insult replaced pleasure.

Eyes closed tight and emotion roiling, she pulled away… then, hauled off and punched him in the arm. The punch served as physical release of the unacceptable tension building inside her.

"Hey!" He rubbed the spot, staring at her in bewilderment.

Horrified at hitting him, especially his pitching arm, she slapped a hand over her mouth. The warmth and moisture of Zak's kiss lingered there, tormenting her. She moved her hand.

"Did I hurt you?"

"What was that for?"

Because I've waited five years for you to wake up, fall in love and kiss me. Because I love you so much I'd almost do something stupid for you. Her family said she was already stupid. Maybe they were right. She had let him kiss her. And she'd kissed him back. Big-time. Maybe she could let down her family. Maybe she could let down herself. But she could never find happiness by betraying her faith.

"You're married."

The shock on his face disappointed her. "No, I'm not." He lifted both hands and then let them drop. "Maybe legally, but that's it."

"That's *it?* You don't consider a vow before God and man as important?"

"You know the circumstances, Jilly. Don't be melodramatic. I don't love, never loved and never felt married to Crystal."

Fighting off the desire to rush right back into his arms and kiss him again, she slammed a hand to her hip. "Well, why don't you tell your excuses to God. This is a moral issue, Zak."

"You're getting riled up," he said, mildly. "Your freckles are going crazy."

Hurt slammed her. Unwanted tears filled her eyes. Jilly pressed cool hands to a red-hot face. Red, being the operative word. "Don't make fun of my freckles."

"Hey." Before she could stop him, Zak had his arms around her. Voice tender, he said, "I love your freckles. Every—" he kissed her cheek "—single—" he kissed her nose "—one—" he kissed her chin. "You're beautiful to me."

Jilly thought her heart might spin out of control and fly right through her rib cage. Her throat filled with a combination of dismay and joy. Love warred with right.

Why did life have to be this complicated?

She wanted to be in Zak's arms, to hear him say she was beautiful in spite of her ugly spots. She wanted to return the kisses and the declaration of love.

A terrible, insidious thought came to her, dangled there like an evil temptation. Crystal was dying. Zak would soon be free.

Horrified that she could think such a thing, she pushed at Zak's chest. "Don't. Please. This is wrong. You know it is. Don't make this any more difficult."

He let her go but didn't step away. Because she wanted him back she crossed her arms to keep them from reaching out.

Zak's hands dangled at his sides, his expression hurt and bewildered. "I can't change the way I feel about you."

She pressed her lips together, aching.

"Me, neither," she said feebly. She couldn't change anything. Her love for him, or her knowledge of right and wrong, or the fact that he had a wife.

Green eyes searched her face. "Can't we at least talk about us?"

"What's to discuss? Crystal's your wife. I'm your friend."

"I don't want to lose you."

Sucking back a threatening sob, she said, "You won't."

He lightened a little and held out a crooked pinky finger. "Promise?"

Reluctantly, she offered hers in a pinky promise. Her skin was cold to his warmth. Truth was, she felt cold to the core.

"BFF," she said with false brightness. Best friends forever. Lovers never.

Both the terriers shot out of the kitchen like rockets.

"Your mom's home. I better go before the rug rats destroy my kingdom. Tell her thanks for the brownies."

"I'll pray about Brandon," Jilly offered. "About what we should do."

"Me, too." He snagged a last brownie and turned to go. "While you're at it, pray about us."

Then he sauntered away, leaving her torn and perplexed and wondering why God had put her in such a painful, unresolvable situation.

Chapter Eleven

Zak figured he'd sunk to an all-time low.

He kicked a stuffed animal out of his path on the way to the refrigerator. Out of habit and a moment of rebellion, he opened the door and swigged from the milk carton. He wanted his life back. He wanted his milk carton and his house and his clean floor back. Most of all, he wanted Jilly.

With a groan, he replaced the milk carton and roamed to the back door. After a glance outside told him the rug rats were continuing the excavation to China, he allowed a few minutes of pity party. Only a small one. He had a game tonight.

When had he fallen in love with Jilly? He didn't know. Maybe he'd loved her forever and was too self-involved to recognize the symptoms. Trouble was, he wasn't sure she returned the feelings. If she did, she wouldn't tell him.

Falling backward onto his couch, he clutched a New York Yankee throw pillow to his face. Had he ruined their friendship? She'd been furious and insulted after he'd kissed her, but he just didn't get her hang-up about Crystal. He wasn't married, not in the real sense. He'd never felt married or considered himself married. Marriage was living together and taking out a mortgage and being there for each other. He and Crystal had never had that. Didn't want it. She'd never been involved in his life. Not like Jilly was. So why was Jilly all stirred about a technicality?

He only had one answer and he didn't like it. Because she was only a friend, and that's all she wanted to be.

He slammed the pillow to the floor, silently apologizing to the Bronx Bombers.

But what about that little "Oh" and the way her blue eyes had lit up and the way she'd melted, just for a minute, against him. What was that all about?

From down the hall, he heard Crystal moving around. She'd been more alert today and had spent time with the kids. He'd been glad for them. They were pitifully tender with their mother and heartrendingly grateful for her attention. It killed him to watch. Before she'd left, Annie said Crystal had eaten a cup of tomato soup and sipped most of a Pepsi. That was good news, wasn't it?

Even his paramedic experience couldn't answer that question for him. Was there such a thing as improvement when a patient was terminal?

A knob rattled and he heard a door open.

"Brandon," Crystal's weak voice called.

Zak shook off his pity party and headed in her direction. She stood in the entry of his guest bedroom, her skin the color of painter's putty.

"Need something?"

"Where's Brandon?"

"Outside. What do you need? You want to see the kids for a while?"

She shook her head. The short curly hair lay flat against her skull. "No, come talk to me."

"You want to sit out here for a change?"

She offered a half smile. "Not sure I can make it that far."

Sympathy swamped him. In three strides he was there,

scooped her up and took her to the living room, taking care not to dislodge the stoppered IV port in her arm. She weighed less than Brandon and felt like a bundle of match sticks. Zak fought a twinge of guilt at being healthy and strong with a long life ahead.

While Zak hovered with pillows to cushion her fragile bones Crystal settled back against the recliner.

"Want something to drink?" She looked as dry as chalk, her lips cracked. Her eyes were glazed and droopy, a sign the morphine was still controlling her pain. He was surprised at her wakefulness.

"Annie left some yuck for me to drink."

"I'll get it." He was back in seconds with a straw and the tepid can of nutrition.

She took one sip, grimaced and returned the can. "Later."

He set the drink aside and wondered what to do with himself. Being with Crystal was awkward at best. He never knew what to say or do.

"Are you going to take my kids?"

She hadn't asked that question in a couple of weeks. His first instinct was to repeat his lack of parenting credentials and tell her he couldn't. But an uncomfortable realization that the rug rats had somehow become important to him stopped him. He thought of Bella's little arms around his neck and Jakey's belly laugh. Even of Brandon's earnest concern for his brother and sister and mother. There was something about those three...

But parent them?

"I don't know," he said, honestly.

"Progress," she muttered. When he arched an eyebrow, she explained, "First time you've not said an outright no."

"Yeah." He looked at her, lying back in the recliner, a fragile shell, and thought of his own healthy body. His ability to run and pitch, the strength in his hands, the freedom from pain. Crystal couldn't walk down a six-foot hall to a chair.

Things like that put life into perspective.

"I'm praying about it," he said.

"You'll be good for them. They love you already."

He shifted, uncomfortable. "I don't know about that."

"I watch you. You care."

Okay, so he did. So the three rug rats had wormed beneath his rib cage and into his heart. A little.

"That doesn't mean I'll be a good parent."

"It's a start." She sighed, tiring visibly. "Don't make them pay for my bad choices. They need an anchor. They need you. I don't want to die not knowing they'll be all right."

"You won't." He wasn't sure what he meant by that, but the pressure of her words was too much for him.

Momentarily, her eyes widened and the morphine glaze disappeared. Behind it shone a desperate hope.

"Jilly?" she said, surprising him.

"You want her to come over? I can call her."

Her eyes dimmed. She let her lids droop shut. "Big heart. Good person."

"Yeah." The best.

"She's crazy about you."

Given the fiasco he'd just left behind at Jilly's house, he found the statement laughable. Kind of. "I don't think so."

"You were always dumb about girls."

"Oh, thanks," he said wryly.

"Such a great-looking guy. Good soul. Too good. Jilly loves you. Trust me. I think you love her, too."

"Yeah." He bounced a fist against his chin. "Maybe."

Who was he fooling? There was no maybe. Once released, this thing inside his heart spilled over into every cell, every pore, every pulse beat. It had taken something as traumatic as Crystal's cancer to open his eyes to what had been right across the street all this time.

"Go for it."

"She's a little hung up on the married thing."

"You'll be a widower soon."

If she'd punched him in the gut, she couldn't have struck him harder. The last thing he wanted to do was feel like a vulture, waiting for someone to die so he could be happy. "Don't do that."

If possible she'd grown paler during their conversation. She seemed determined to talk, but the effort was taking a toll.

"Are you hurting?" he asked, digging out his cell, ready to call Annie back.

"Exhausted." A sad grimace of a smile tilted one side of her mouth. "Never thought I'd be too tired to talk to a cute guy. So not fun."

There was nothing fun about her life now. Nothing left for her but drugged pain relief and the hope that he would take care of her children.

If he agreed, his life would change forever. He didn't want his life to change. Other than Jilly. He wanted her, although he'd never have her if he agreed to Crystal's wild request. What single, beautiful woman wanted to take on three troubled children? He was having a hard enough time with it. Why would he ask someone he cared about to make the same sacrifice?

If what Crystal said was true? If Jilly loved him, too?

How did a man make such a momentous decision?

Pastor Parker dropped by the next morning, a visit that provoked mixed feelings in Zak. On the one hand, the preacher's appearance embarrassed him, although he wasn't sure why—maybe the unorthodox and completely unspiritual issue of his marriage. On the other hand, the pastor was a friend and a spiritual guide. If ever Zak had needed both, it was today.

The pastor, who made weekly pilgrimages to visit Crystal, was a genial man around forty with yellow hair and an outdoorsman's ruddy complexion. Brandon let him in without so much as a greeting. Zak, still wiping pancake syrup from the table, chairs and cabinets, poked his head around the door facing. "Go on back, pastor. Annie's with her."

Pastor Parker waved acknowledgment and started off down the hall.

Zak continued de-syruping the potted plant Jilly had given him for Valentine's Day. He loved that plant, a twisted little cactus he seldom remembered to water, which made the plant and him perfectly happy. Jilly knew him well.

By the time Pastor Parker completed his time with Crystal, the kids had helped clean up the kitchen. Even Bella was learning to put her own dish in the dishwasher and pick up her toys. Most of the time.

"Got a minute, Zak?" the pastor asked.

Zak rinsed the sponge. "Sure." To the rug rats he said, "You can go outside and play now. Stay in the yard. Hear me, Brandon?"

Every time he let the kid out of his sight, Brandon disappeared. Even though tempted to give the bicycle back to GI Jack, he didn't have the heart to take anything else away from the wounded boy. He had, on the other hand, made a few phone calls and had discovered a juvenile firesetters intervention program run by the county. Just in case he needed it.

The back door vibrated as the trio blasted outside. Watching them, Zak grinned. He loved the outside, too, would rather be there than inside anytime.

"Coffee?" he asked, hitching his chin toward the still-fresh pot.

"Wouldn't say no if you'll have one with me."

Zak went for the cups. "Be careful where you sit. I think we sponged up all the syrup, but you never know."

The minister smiled knowingly. "Pancakes, huh?"

"The kids like them." The fresh aroma of coffee wafted upward as he poured from the carafe with one hand and reached for the sugar bowl with the other. "Bella had never had a pancake before, so you can imagine the mess she made with syrup."

Pastor took the offered earthenware mug and made himself comfortable at the freshly scrubbed table. Moisture still gleamed from the top. Zak hoped it was only water and not more syrup. "Toddlers are messy."

"How was I to know she couldn't handle a squirt bottle?" Sitting down with his brew, Zak grinned at his own ignorance. "I guess Crystal hasn't been up to cooking for a long time."

Truth was he'd never known her to cook anything but macaroni and cheese and frozen pizza.

"How are things going otherwise, Zak? You've taken on quite a challenge. You doing okay?"

"Surviving." He blew the steam away from his cup. "I don't know what I'm doing half the time and when I'm gone to work or a game, I worry something will happen."

"Tough situation." The preacher dumped a packet of sweetener into his cup. "Crystal asked me to talk to you."

"About the kids."

"Yes."

"She's terrified of them going into foster care."

Pastor Parker swirled a spoon round and round the steaming liquid. "She told me about her early life."

"Then you know. But I'm not sure I can raise three kids," Zak said honestly. "Any sage advice?"

"You're the only one, with God whispering in your ear, who can make that decision."

The answer wasn't all that helpful, but Zak appreciated the effort just the same. "Thanks for not pushing."

Pastor lifted his coffee in acknowledgment, sipped once and set it down again. "Something else Crystal said…not that it's any of my business…but I'm willing to listen if you want to talk about it." Zak blinked, unsure of his meaning until he said, "Jilly Fairmont."

A pain struck Zak in the left chest, right where his heart was supposed to be. With a sigh, he shoved his mug aside and perched his elbows on the table. "I love her."

He could tell by the slight narrowing of the preacher's clear, hazel eyes that he understood the issues involved in making such a statement. "How does she feel?"

"I don't know." Images of Jilly cascaded through his head. Jilly and him popping popcorn and throwing chips at each other during commercials. Jilly in his house, at his games, beside him in church. For five years, she'd been omnipresent in his life. He waved off the statement. "Not completely true. I've taken her for granted and never realized how important she is to me. I thought we were best friends, but now I wonder if it was more all along and I was too—" he shrugged, ashamed "—self-focused, I guess, to notice."

"Have you told Jilly these things?"

"Some. She knows I'm in love with her." He hadn't meant to blurt the words, but they'd jumped out of his heart and over his tongue faster than his brain could reel them back in.

"And?" Pastor Parker was a man's man, not some milquetoast preacher who didn't understand life. He had a family, raised farm animals, shepherded a large flock of believers. And Zak trusted him implicitly.

"She's freaked out about my relationship with Crystal." He picked up a spoon, stared at his muddy reflection in the metal and put it down again. "That's the tough part, Pastor. I don't know what's right and wrong in this situation. I don't want to compromise my faith or Jilly's, but I don't feel married to Crystal. I never did. You know the situation. You know why I married her back in college. Is it wrong for me and Jilly to be together when a piece of ancient history says I'm married to someone else?"

The preacher grew quiet, his gaze focused on the back-yard. Beyond the patio doors, the voices of three children carried into the cozy kitchen, reminders of the decisions hanging in the balance. Could he keep those kids and have Jilly, too? Dare he even consider such a thing?

And what about Crystal?

"Your situation is unique, Zak," the pastor said. "Not that something like this is a first for God, but it is for me. From all you and Crystal have said, this is a gray area with no absolute answer from scripture that I can bring to mind. You're married to Crystal, a woman you barely know, but you're in love with Jilly and I suspect she's in love with you, too."

That perked him up. "You think?"

"We men are usually the last to figure out these things, but my wife suspected it long ago."

"She did?" Just how long had he been blind to Jilly?

"This is a heart problem, Zak, a matter of conscience, and only you and God can decide what's right."

"I don't want to wish Crystal's life away."

"Seeing what you've done here, no one would think such a thing."

He let out a big sigh of relief. "Thank you for that. Sometimes I wake in the night with my heart pounding, afraid of Crystal dying, afraid of being left with her kids and afraid of losing Jilly, too. I don't know what to feel anymore."

The pastor finished off his coffee, settling the mug with a clunk of ceramic against wood. "Even though I can't give you an absolute answer to the situation, I can promise you this. Fear and anxiety are not from God."

Zak knew that. What he didn't know was, "How do I get past them?"

"I won't pat you on the head and tell you there are easy answers to any of this, but I find prayer the most direct road to peace."

Zak nodded, convinced the pastor was correct but frustrated that his prayers seemed ineffective. His faith had always come easy and naturally. Lately, not so much. "Will you pray for me? For us?"

"How about right now?"

"Thanks." Zak swallowed, gratitude filling his throat as he bowed his head.

After the preacher left, Zak rewarmed his coffee and sat at the table, his Bible open and his heart lifted in prayer. After a while, he closed the book and put his head in his hands. If God had an answer, He wasn't sharing.

Chapter Twelve

❧

The kids found the baby bird Friday evening. They'd been playing in Jilly's backyard with the bunnies for nearly an hour, their giggles and antics bringing energetic joy to the usually quiet area. Mom was at her knitting club, having left in a huff with a reminder that those kids were Zak's responsibility and Amber was right, Jilly was letting him take advantage.

Mom helped out with the kids, too, but she never saw that as the same, a situation that annoyed Jilly and hurt her feelings. For Mother, caring for Crystal's children was altruism. For Jilly, according to her family, it was a pathetic attempt to somehow win Zak's love.

She didn't want Zak's love. Could they understand that?

No, that wasn't exactly true. She wanted to love him. She just didn't want to displease God.

"Anyone thirsty? I have popsicles." More evidence of what a doormat she was.

"Popsicles," Jakey cried, leaping up as though she'd promised a trip to Disney World.

"I'll bring them out." She jogged inside, pulled the homemade treats from the freezer, grabbed a roll of paper towels and headed back out. If there was one thing she'd learned, wet wipes and paper towels were a must for anyone with kids.

The last thought made her brain stutter. They weren't her kids, as Mom liked to point out. Would she mind if they were? Could she be a mother to three older children?

Scary. And yet...

"Jilly, come quick. Hurry." Brandon and the other two were in the corner of the yard beneath a giant apple tree that hung over the fence from the alley. They squatted on the grass and formed a circle around something.

The three rabbits hopped around the trio of kids, secure that Jilly never let them out with the terriers. Not that she thought Mugsy or Satchmo would harm the bunnies, but she wasn't taking a chance.

"What's wrong?"

"A baby bird." Before she could tell him not to, Brandon had scooped the little creature into his palm and started toward her. "He's hurt. He fell."

All four tilted their heads upward to find the nest high above. Jilly's heart dipped. The baby had tumbled at least ten feet.

"You can fix him, can't you, Jilly?" Jakey asked, doing his best not to stick his thumb in his mouth. She handed him a popsicle. "You're a doctor. You can fix him."

She didn't bother to correct him. The children knew she worked at the vet clinic, wore scrubs most of the time, and to them, she was a doctor. "I don't know, Jake. He's really young to have fallen so far. And he appears injured."

The bird's pulsating heart pushed at the thin blue skin barely covering his tiny chest. One wing twisted upward. His neck was floppy, his yellow beak open in soundless distress.

"He can't die. You can't let him." Anger burned in Brandon's brown eyes. Anger and something else. Fear. "It wouldn't be fair. He's a good bird. He didn't do anything wrong."

With heart aching, Jilly handed each child a cherry popsicle and then reached for the bird. As Brandon transferred him into her palm, the tiny creature's heart stopped its frantic beating.

"He's dead." Brandon spun around, storming to the fence where he slammed his fist into the hardwood. Red popsicle juice splattered the gray boards like blood.

Jilly gently placed the dead bird on the rabbit hutch and went to the boy. Bella and Jake followed.

"Everything dies." He kept his back turned, but tears muffled his words. "I hate it. I hate everything. It's not fair."

Jilly did what came naturally. She went down on her knees beside him and slid an arm around his waist, urging him to lean on her. He stood stiff as the fence, resistant, tears streaming down his face.

"Don't cry, Brandon." Bella pushed her popsicle at him.

He pushed it back. "I'm not crying."

The two little ones stood stricken, whether by the death of the bird or by the sight of their older, controlled brother crying, she didn't know.

"I'm sorry, Brandon. I know this is hard. Everything in your world right now is confusing and difficult to understand." She saw the parallels and knew Brandon cried as much for his mother as he did for the bird. "I feel helpless, too, but you know what helps me?"

He cut his eyes toward her and sniffed. "What?"

"I talk to Jesus and tell Him all about it. He went through some hard times, too, and lost people He loved. He understands how much that hurts."

"They killed him for being nice. Nice people always die."

"Jesus *gave* Himself. No one killed Him. He let them hurt Him that way so He'd know how you feel." She was simplifying for a child's understanding while praying to give Brandon something real to cling to. "That's why He understands. You can tell Him anything."

How could a small child comprehend the power of Christ's peace? How could she give them what they needed when she wasn't even sure what it was?

"Jesus," she said aloud, feeling foolish but believing she had to do something for these hurting children. "Brandon and Jake and Bella need You. Please help them. Show me what to do and say. Let them feel your comfort and love. Your Bible says You see every little sparrow that falls to the ground. You care about everything." She paused, took a breath, praying inwardly that the rest of her prayer would not upset them. "Lord, please, more than anything, let them know their mother will be with You and she'll be all right."

She was uncertain of Crystal's spiritual condition, but today the children needed hope and this was all she could give them.

"Can we bury him?" Brandon asked, interrupting.

Jilly blinked, the prayer gone, replaced by an idea that could possibly prepare the children for the days ahead. With solemn dignity, they found an appropriate box—after emptying tea bags into a plastic baggie—and lined it with soft grass. Jake insisted they walk in a line out the back door to a spot behind the rabbit hutch they'd chosen as the burial site. Brandon, his narrow shoulders hunching, insisted on digging the grave.

Once the box was lowered into the freshly turned ground, Jake said, "We're 'sposed to sing now."

He'd been watching *Little House on the Prairie.*

Bella clapped her hands and started, "I'm in the Lord's Army," a song they'd learned in Bible school. And even though Jilly was amused, she was also touched and wouldn't have laughed if her life depended on it. The three solemn faces sang from the heart, pumped their arms and marched in place over the small grave site.

At the conclusion, they all looked to Jilly, then bowed their heads. The sweetness brought a lump to her throat. They'd never been to church until their arrival in Redemption, until Zak had started taking them every week and had sent them to Vacation Bible School. But their little spirits craved the promise of heaven, the hope of something better and bigger and more loving then life had been so far.

"Pray, Brandon," Jake said.

Brandon clasped his hands under his chin and, sounding a lot like Pastor Parker, said, "God, here's this bird. You made him. Take him to heaven so he can fly and not be hurt anymore. Amen."

Amen. Take him to heaven so he can fly and not hurt.

With solemn care, each child placed a pansy, picked from Mom's flower bed, on the mound of dirt. Bella bent and kissed the dirt. "Bye, little bird."

"Come on, Bella," Jake said, being a big boy. "He'll be all right now. He's with Jesus."

Tears prickled behind Jilly's eyelids. She turned away to see Zak standing at the corner of the house, watching.

Sunday morning, the backyard funeral scene continued to roll around in Zak's head. Jilly had explained the situation over hot dogs grilled in his backyard, an event he considered as progress. All the time they'd grilled and pretended to be nothing but friends, he kept thinking about how she always knew the right thing to do. The kids went to her, trusted her. So did he. She'd make a great mother.

He shifted on the pew to rub his pitching arm. Last night's game had left him achy. The Rogues had won, though, thanks to his achy arm and fastball. He'd have to ice his elbow this afternoon and lie on the couch in front of the Yankees game. Anyway, that's what he'd have done B.C., before Crystal.

The drummer clacked his drum sticks together and the worship team kicked into a happy praise song.

Zak felt lonely this morning with the kids in children's church and Jilly careful not to sit beside him. She sat with her mother two rows ahead where he was tantalized by the bouncy bob of penny-colored hair and the pretty splash of matching freckles on the back of her neck.

He had the completely unspiritual thought that he'd like to kiss those freckles. Wonder what she'd do if he did?

What would it be like to sit beside her in church and belong together, to have a right to kiss her neck? Was he, as she claimed, wrong to think this way?

He rose with the congregation and clapped his hands to the beat, trying to focus on worship instead of Jilly.

Lately, his prayers hit the ceiling and bounced back in his face. Distraction would cause that he supposed. He sure wasn't blaming God. Their relationship had been easy for a long time. Not so much these days.

As the song ended, GI Jack and Popbottle Jones slipped into the pew beside him. He nodded a greeting, glad for their company but surprised they were late.

When the message began, the preacher took his text from the book of Mark, the Garden of Gethsemane scene most everyone in the church knew well. But instead of the usual discussion of Christ's agony, Pastor Parker titled his message, "Doing the hard stuff."

"And He went forward a little, and fell on the ground, and prayed that if it were possible, the hour might pass from Him," Pastor Parker read as Zak watched the giant screen on the wall and read along. "And He said, Abba, Father, all things are possible unto thee; take away this cup from me: nevertheless not what I will, but what thou wilt."

It struck Zak then, that he'd been praying for God to remove his problem, but he'd never once considered accepting them as Christ had been willing to do.

"All of us face hard situations in life," Pastor Parker said. "We're asked to do the hard stuff, to make a difficult decision that doesn't feel good to our flesh, just as Jesus was. Will your answer be, 'Thy will, Lord' Or will you say, 'No, not me. Get someone else.'?"

Zak shifted on the padded pew, stirred by the words. He was being asked to raise Crystal's children and he'd searched for someone else to take the responsibility. He hadn't been willing to do the hard stuff.

But he had a life, he argued inwardly. He had a job. He had things he wanted to do that did not include three orphaned children.

"An important thing to remember about these verses is this. Anytime you follow God's path and deny your own will, blessing awaits you." The pastor smiled, his yellow hair shiny beneath the podium lights. "Don't miss out on a blessing. If God asks, say yes. Do the hard stuff. And reap the joy of the Lord and His great rewards."

Great rewards. Could Crystal's kids be considered rewards?

The answer came, a faint whisper, a gentle breeze that blew across his conscience and his heart. If he did the hard thing. If he handled them right. If he dared to trust in what he now understood to be right. Warts and all, Brandon, Bella and Jake could be the greatest blessing of his life.

"I called Hunter Case after church. He'll be here Tuesday morning when I get off shift."

"Weird time of day for a game of catch," Jilly said, grinning. "What's up?"

His belly quivered a little when he looked at her now.

Now that he knew he loved her. Now that he wanted to be with her all the time. Now that he found reasons to touch her. Casually, of course. A brush of the hand, a squeeze on her shoulder, the bump of bodies preparing a meal over his grill.

That's where they were this afternoon. The kids ran the makeshift baseball field he'd built in his backyard, sliding, pushing and yelling the way kids do. Jilly's terriers leaped and raced, tongues wagging with delight at having three children to play with. The scents of hot dog and mesquite wood filled the air and made his belly growl.

"Watch this, Zak," Jake yelled as he tossed the ball up and smacked it with a fat plastic bat. At the hit, Bella raced toward first base but got distracted and headed for the outfield and a dandelion instead.

"Good rip, Jake," Jilly called, pumping her fist in the air and hollering. "Woo-hoo!"

Serious-faced Brandon wasn't to be ignored. Using one of Zak's dented metal bats he slammed a ground ball toward the alley, raced to the cardboard "first" before turning expectantly.

"Awesome, dude," Zak acknowledged and was rewarded with a smile.

Rewarded. Were these the kinds of rewards the preacher had meant? Small joys of a smile, a hit ball, a little girl bringing him a dandelion and the simple feeling of happiness that glowed in his chest?

He checked the browning hot dogs and then laid the giant fork on the edge of the grill. His pulse jittered some, but he was certain he was making the right choice. Would Jilly agree? "I'm taking custody of the kids."

Jilly whirled toward him, mouth working, eyes wide and surprised.

"Zak," she said. And then she hugged him. "Oh, Zak, that's fabulous."

Her breath warmed his left ear and his brain disconnected. For a nanosecond, he didn't think about the kids or custody or Crystal. He thought about Jilly. How good she smelled, like mesquite smoke and clean flowery perfume, and how good she felt in his arms again. He kissed the side of her head, the tickle of her red hair welcome against his skin.

This was joy as well. A woman to love.

"Jilly," he said, trying not to cross her line in the sand although the restraint cost him. He tightened his arms and then released her with a laugh. "If I'd known I'd get that kind of reaction, I would have called Hunter weeks ago."

"Have you told Crystal? What made you decide?" She was all glowy, her peach skin flushed prettily, her adorable freckles tempting him to touch.

Fingers itchy, he tapped her cheek, let his fingertips linger. "Yes to the first."

"Was she thrilled?"

"Relieved, I think."

He'd expected something different than Crystal's reaction. She'd stared at him for one long moment, nodded and said a quiet thanks. Then she'd closed her eyes and shut him out. A tear slipped from the corner of one eye, a fact that puzzled him.

He told Jilly.

"I think I know why, Zak. She's relieved but at the same time, having her children settled with you brings back the fact she won't be here for them."

"Yeah, I guess you're right." He hooked a casual arm over her shoulders. "See why I love you? You're brilliant."

She ducked away and pointed a finger at him, eyes narrowed in warning, although he saw the humor lurking, too. "Be good or I'll go home."

He lifted both hands in surrender. "Can't blame a guy for trying."

She turned away, crinkled the package of hot dog buns. Her behavior maddened him. Just once, he wanted her to admit she cared for him, too.

"What time is your game?" She squirted yellow mustard in long strips on five opened buns.

"Seven." He forked a frank and deposited it on the bun. "We play here, so I'll head over to the field about six. You're coming, aren't you?"

Instead of answering, she said, "Do the other players make comments about me being there?"

He frowned, puzzled. "Comments? Why would they do that? Other than to say you look really fine in shorts, but hey, they're guys, what do you expect?"

"I'm serious, Zak." She folded a bun and added a handful of potato chips to the plate. "Do they make comments about me being with you when you have a wife?"

Oh. Now he got it.

"They understand about Crystal." At least, he assumed they did. Other than Hunter and a couple of other close buddies, no one said anything at all about his weird situation. Gossip handled the rest.

"Do they know about—" She stopped, bit her lip, flashed him a blue worried glance. "Me? Us?"

"Is there an us?" His pulse elevated.

"There can't be."

Exasperating woman. "You're driving me nuts, Jilly." He moved behind her, lifted the swing of red hair from her neck and kissed her freckles. There. He'd done it. She could punch him if she wanted, but he'd kissed her. For good measure, he did it again.

She shivered. "Zak, stop." But the words were feeble and he heard the longing in her voice, a longing that matched the one in his heart.

"Don't feel guilty," he whispered.

"Don't make me guilty," she answered. "My mom does enough of that already."

He stepped away, stricken. The last thing he wanted was to cause Jilly grief. Without her, he couldn't have gotten through these past weeks.

Zak sighed, resigned to let it go for now.

"Promise you won't abandon me in my time of need." *Promise to love me, to never leave me, no matter how crazy my life becomes.* But he didn't say those things. Jilly would bolt if he did. Selfish as it was, he needed her, especially during the upcoming conversation with three scared children.

She gazed at him for one long beat. "I probably should, but I can't."

Zak found her hand and held tight, relieved when she didn't pull away.

"Will you—" he swallowed, blew out an anxious breath "—help me tell the kids about the guardianship?"

She laced her fingers with his and squeezed. "Scared?"

"A big, tough fireman like me? Scared? Not even close. I'm terrified."

Chapter Thirteen

Call her crazy, but Jilly took off from work on Tuesday morning to be with Zak, the children and Crystal. The scene was poignant—the dying mother and grieving children accepting of what had to be. Once Crystal's shaky hand had signed the papers, Jilly and Annie signed as witnesses and Hunter Case's accompanying assistant notarized them. And the deed was done.

Taking less than fifteen minutes, the change of guardianship from Crystal to Zak seemed almost anticlimactic.

"Congratulations. You're a father." Hunter slapped Zak on the back as he and his aide left. Zak stood in the doorway, looking stunned.

Jilly felt for him. "You're going to be fine."

"But what about the kids?"

The two of them had walked the legal eagles to the door, leaving Crystal and her children alone for a while.

"They seemed stoically accepting," she told him. "At least now they won't be worrying about what's going to happen to them after..."

"Did they ever ask you about that?"

"Some."

"Me, too." He took a deep breath, shook his head like a

prize fighter warding off a blow and came toward her. "I don't want them to be scared anymore. But they are. Their mother is dying and I can't fix that by signing a piece of paper."

"You said they were doing better, and Bella's almost potty trained."

"Jake's still sucking his thumb at night, but he's not crying as much."

"You're a stabilizing factor."

"Poor kids. Stuck with me for stability. Scary." But he grinned when he said it. Then his face grew serious and he slithered onto a chair. "I'm officially an adult. What if I can't do it? What if I mess them up and they grow up to be maniacs or drug addicts or bums?"

"What if they don't? No parent knows the answers to those questions. Sometimes you have to trust God to work things out."

"Easy for you to say. You get to go home to your terriers."

But she didn't want to. "And if they act up, I toss them out in the backyard."

"I do the same with the kids."

They exchanged looks. A slow smile built inside Jilly and was reflected on Zak's face. Then both broke out laughing at the silly statement.

Maybe it was the seriousness of the day, the heavy burden of stress hanging over the household, but they needed to laugh. The release was all out of proportion to the event, but still they laughed until somehow, Jilly was leaning into Zak's side, and he was holding her up with one arm.

Tears trickled down her face and her throat hurt. When she looked up, three curious faces stared at her.

"What's funny?" Brandon asked, looking angry.

"Nothing. We're just being silly." Instantly, she regretted the words. Today wasn't a day to be silly. Was it?

"Are we supposed to call you dad now?" Jake said to Zak, the furrow between his eyebrows deeper than usual.

Jilly saw the quick sobering on Zak's face, felt his body stiffen.

"What do you want to call me?"

Jake cocked his head to one side. "Are you my dad?"

"Not technically."

How did he explain the complicated relationship between their mother and himself? Jilly didn't think he could. A least not for a long time.

"Mom said you're our dad now."

Zak's mouth opened and closed without saying a word.

"I'm not calling you dad. You're not my dad." Brandon reached for Bella. "Come on, let's go play ball."

Bella jerked away to wrap her small arm around Zak's knee. "I want Dad play ball."

"Me, too," Jake said, chin jutting stubbornly. "Dad and us."

Jilly's throat filled with emotion when Brandon hitched one shoulder and said, "Come on, then."

Zak scooped Bella into his big pitcher's hands and tossed her easily onto his shoulders. She squealed, giggled and grabbed his ears to hold on.

"You coming?" he asked Jilly.

Something changed in the room then, a subtle shift from three kids and a willing guardian to a fledgling family. A family to which she couldn't belong.

"You go ahead. I want to say something to Crystal first."

With Bella thumping his sides with her heels, Zak galloped through the kitchen and out of sight.

The fire started on the outskirts of town in an older neighborhood of wide lawns and deep, secret alleys littered with overhanging trees and outbuildings. By the time Zak and B Crew arrived on the scene, the flames had spread to a large garden area, neglected this season because of the drought.

As taught in the academy, the crew set up to "attack from the black," a means of keeping firefighters and equipment out of danger as much as possible.

Zak manned a four-inch hose, thankful for the fire hydrant half a block away. The stench of burning wood and old junk filled his lungs. Working his way along the edge of the blaze, he caught sight of onlookers from the neighboring homes, many of whom he knew, at least by name.

Flames shot high into the air and caught quick hold of a dilapidated and empty chicken coop. His walkie-talkie crackled and Captain's voice said, "Ashford, work your way around to the back of that coop. Billings, stay in the front and keep the flames from moving toward the north residence."

"Yes, sir," Zak replied, moving as he spoke. He reached the back of the ramshackle building, relieved to report the fire was contained in the front for the moment. He hosed down the surrounding grass and shrubs and had started back around when something blue and shiny flashed in the sunlight. At the far end of the alley almost hidden behind a giant magnolia sat a blue bicycle.

Zak's heart lurched. Brandon's dark hair and slight form were unmistakable. Worse, the moment the bike rider realized the firefighter was staring in his direction, he mounted the bike and pedaled rapidly away.

Sickness rolled in Zak's stomach. He'd prayed to be wrong, still hoped he was.

His radio crackled and he followed the captain's commands, going through the motions like the well-trained firefighter he was. As soon as the flames were controlled, he went to his captain.

"I need a couple of hours, Captain."

Captain Porter looked him over. "You okay?"

"Physically, yes." Zak rubbed the sleeve of his jacket over his face. He was covered in soot. "I have something at home that needs my attention now. I need only an hour or two."

Captain studied him for a moment before saying, "Take the rest of the day. Let me know if I can help."

"Thanks, Captain." The truth of the business was Zak had no idea what to do if his suspicions were correct. The only thing he knew for certain was that Brandon was his responsibility.

Right now, that responsibility hung heavy on his shoulders.

"What were you doing at the fire today?" Zak stood over Brandon, hands on his hips, aware of how intimidating he must look to a nine-year-old with his face covered in ash and soot. Still in stinking turnout gear, he hoped the vision was enough to shake the truth out of the boy.

Brandon sat on the couch watching aliens invade the world. When he didn't look up, Zak stepped in front of the TV and took the remote, wondering if aliens had invaded his world, too.

Fear flashed on Brandon's face for one infinitesimal moment before he looked way and muttered, "I don't know what you're talking about."

The blatant lie stoked Zak's anger and worry. He was so churned up that he said the first things that came into his head. "I saw you there, on your bike at the end of the alley. Don't lie to me. Not now, not ever. Did you start that fire?"

Brandon flew up from the sofa, fists clenched at his sides. "Leave me alone. I hate you."

Before Zak could stop him, he bolted for the door and

slammed outside. Jake and Bella came down the hall, eyes wide.

"Brandon's mad," Jake said.

Zak sank onto the couch and scrubbed his face with his hands, reluctant to give chase. At least, not yet. He needed to get a grip and consider the proper way to talk to a troubled kid.

Hands clasped together against his forehead, he leaned his elbows on his knees and prayed silently. *Help me, Lord. I'm drowning. I don't know what to do with any kid much less a troubled one. Anyone would be better at this than me.*

A small hand patted his knee. "It's okay, Zak."

He raised his head to the sight of Bella's blond head leaning in to kiss his filthy hand. His aching heart turned over.

"You two stay here, okay? I'm going to find Brandon."

"He's probably at Jilly's," Jake said. "He always goes there when he's mad."

Jilly's. She was better at this kid thing than he was. "Thanks, Jake. Watch your sister, okay?"

"Annie's here."

"I know." He didn't know what he would do without neighbors and Annie. Even though Annie's job was hospice care for Crystal, as a friend she kept an eye on the children, too, as much as she could. Grimly, he realized, someone needed to be with them all the time. The home-alone syndrome was not working out too well for Brandon.

Jilly saw him coming and opened the door before he knocked. Still in gear, minus the black-and-yellow jacket, he looked dirty and exhausted, and every cell in her body reached out to him.

He was going through a rough patch, as her father used to say.

"You look fried," she said. "Please don't tell me there was another grass fire."

"Yeah." His shoulders sagged. "I saw Brandon there."

She made a small sound of distress. "He's in the back with the rabbits. I saw him go around a few minutes ago."

"Thanks." He nodded wearily and started off the porch.

He hadn't asked for her help. He hadn't tried to touch her or change her mind about their relationship, but the memory of being held against that strong firefighter chest, of watching him take on the responsibility of three small children, stirred her to action. He needed her. He was just too proud to ask.

The door creaked as she stepped out on the porch. On this Wednesday, her afternoon off from the clinic, she and Mom had been baking for the church bake sale and the aroma of chocolate chip cookies clung to her the way fire stench clung to Zak.

"You want company?" she asked softly, wondering if she'd regret the question later but determined to be the friend he needed. He and Brandon both needed a friend today.

A face ringed in black turned to look over one shoulder. "I need *you*."

The way he said it pulled at her with the strength of gravity. Zak needed her.

She gave one nod and fell into step beside him, painfully aware of how much she loved him and how much she'd sacrifice to be with him. Now that he'd said he loved her, it grew harder and harder to keep him at arm's length. She wanted to be with him, to help him carry the heavy burden he was under.

They rounded the house to open the side gate leading into the Fairmont backyard. Brandon, a lop-eared rabbit in his lap, watched their approach with a sullen expression.

Lucky the lop wiggled at the sight of Jilly, whiskers flicking and nose quivering. Brandon stroked the rabbit's back.

"Can we talk?" Zak asked, going to one knee.

Jilly settled on the grass next to Brandon, using the rabbit as an excuse to sit close to the boy.

Brandon shrugged, eyes on the lop, and said nothing.

The adults exchanged glances. Worry hung on Zak like the stench of fire.

"Brandon," he said. "I'm not trying to scare you but we have to talk about this. I saw you at the fire."

Gently, Jilly asked, "Why were you there, Brandon? Please tell us. We want to help."

"Nothing you can do." He sank deeper into himself, head lowered to the rabbit so that his voice was barely distinguishable. "Nothing anyone can do."

Jilly strongly suspected Brandon was talking about more than the fires. Apparently, so did Zak. He touched Brandon's folded knee.

"Life is lousy for you right now, buddy," Zak said. "Don't make it worse. Your mom needs to know you're going to be okay."

"Don't tell her."

Jilly met Zak's gaze and read the questions there. "Don't tell her what?"

The boy shrugged. "Nothing."

"We want to make things better, Brandon," Jilly said, "but you have to tell us the truth."

Zak scratched the rabbit's ear, but Jilly could see his mind was on Brandon. "Did you start that fire? If you did, tell me. We can work this out."

"Will I be in trouble?"

Finally some progress.

"Brandon," she said, "I think what Zak is saying is that

he knows people to talk to and people who will understand and help you."

Brandon thrust out a stubborn chin, but his eyes glistened suspiciously. "Will I have to go jail?"

Heavy cloth rustled as Zak moved in close to the boy's side and wrapped a long arm around his shoulders. "No."

The slim face looked up at the man, trusting but afraid. "You sure? Mama would cry if I went to jail like my dad. He made her cry."

Jilly's stomach hurt for the little boy who'd been through too much.

"I'm positive. They won't put you in jail, but you have to tell the truth. Did you set that fire?"

The child drew in a deep breath and shuddered before admitting in a small, frightened voice, "Yes."

Zak pulled him a little closer. "You're a good boy, Brandon. We're going to get through this together. Okay?"

Brandon nodded and for the first time since she'd known him, he not only didn't shy away from Zak's touch, but he also leaned in closer and rested his head on the fireman's strong shoulder.

Zak kissed the top of his head and then rested his cheek on the boy's hair.

If Jilly hadn't loved her neighbor before, she would have then. Like a good father, he would insist his son take responsibility for his actions, but he would be with him all the way.

Chapter Fourteen

"Come over. Hurry."

Brandon's breathless request was like an electric jolt, fueling Jilly's worry that something else had gone wrong in the house across the street.

"What is it?" Jilly stepped out on the porch.

"Just come. You gotta see."

The little boy's pleas brought her mother to the door, too. "What in the world? Brandon, is someone hurt?"

"No." He shook his head and the grin he'd been holding back broke through.

Jilly stared, amazed and blessed. This was progress indeed. "Something good must have happened."

He grabbed her hand. "Yeah. Come on."

With a backward glance at her mother's troubled expression, Jilly allowed Brandon to pull her down the incline. She'd received a lecture that very morning about her "hopeless clinging" to the man next door. She knew her mother was right, but Brandon was a hurting child and he had few enough joys. Should she refuse him just because he lived with Zak?

Through the sun-washed evening they jogged across the drying grass and around Zak's house to the backyard. Jilly heard shouts of glee long before she saw the reason for the excitement.

"Look, Jilly, Zak bought a swing and a slide and everything."

Sure enough, Zak and a couple of his friends were putting together a playground set, complete with a wooden fort above the slide. Half the set was erected with the other half strung around the yard like the aftermath of a whirlwind.

"Wow!"

Zak looked up from his work, grinning like the kids. "Cool, huh?"

"Awesome." *Like you.* 'Hi, Brent. Jeff. Nice of you to help."

"Blackmail," Brent said, wielding a screwdriver. "We had to make sure he didn't miss another ballgame. We play at seven."

"Ah, I see. Clever of you." She steadied the metal pole while he connected the washer and bolt. Zak hadn't said a word about the game tonight. What was he planning to do? Wait until the last minute and ask her to go with him? Or to babysit the kids? Mom's warnings, still fresh in her head, came again. If she mattered, he would have told her ahead of time instead of expecting her to drop everything the moment he realized his need.

"Looks great." She turned loose of the pole and stepped away. "I have to get back home. Have fun."

Metal clanged as Zak dropped a wrench and came toward her. "Wait a minute."

She paused. "What?"

"Where are you going?"

When he looked clueless and cute this way, she struggled not to give in, especially because she wanted to. "Home. I have things to do before work tomorrow."

He scratched the side of his head, frowning. "Are you coming to the game?"

"No." *And if you ask me who's going to watch the rug rats while you play, I might become violent.*

"I was hoping we could talk." He wrapped his fingers around her elbow. At his touch, her hurt softened. Zak was Zak and he didn't have a mean bone in his body. If he took her for granted, it was her fault.

"About what?"

"Brandon. I signed us up for the county's juvenile fire-setter intervention program."

Jilly blinked. "I didn't know such a thing existed."

"My captain suggested it. I knew about the program, but I guess my head's been in other places."

"Go figure."

"Yeah." Idly, his fingers massaged her elbow in circles. He'd always done that kind of thing, but it felt different now, a forbidden pleasure. "I took him to the first class last night. It was good. He learned a lot. So did I, about how to handle him, what to do so this doesn't become a permanent problem. They even have a psychologist who'll be counseling him every week."

"An answer to prayer." With regret she eased her arm from his touch.

"Absolutely." His hand dropped. He stood, looking awkward and uncomfortable. They'd never been uncomfortable with each other. "You okay? You're acting funny."

Forcing a smile, she started walking again. She was glad he'd found counsel for Brandon, although a weekly program was one more reason to use her babysitter service. The merry-go-round of neediness never ended. Before Crystal, she hadn't minded. Before, when she and Zak had shared all kinds of things and she'd received as much as she'd given.

Sometimes now she felt as used as her sisters claimed she was.

Was she being selfish?

"Tired," she said, head down, aware of his Converse slip-ons keeping pace, and even more aware of the man wearing them.

"Mrs. Bertram's St. Bernard must have come in for a bath and clip," he teased as they came around the side of the house.

"Something like that." He shouldn't walk with her. She wished he wouldn't. Then, she wished he would. People would criticize, especially her family. Ugh, she was driving herself crazy. "Trace and Cheyenne are going to have a baby."

Zak paused at the corner of the house, his face twisted in bewilderment. "Is that a bad thing?"

"No. I just happened to think of it." Yet, while she'd been thrilled for her friends, a tiny part of her had been jealous, which was completely ridiculous. Trace and Cheyenne had both had their share of heartaches and difficult times. They'd worked hard to build a strong home and family together. She didn't begrudge them, but she wanted a family, too.

She should have kept walking. She should have gone back across the street to her terriers and her rabbits. But she didn't. She stood at the side of Zak's house, with the sound of playing children and conversing males in the background, yearning for a lanky firefighter with too much on his plate.

He took a step closer. Her heart clutched but she stood her ground. What else could she do with a wall of brick less than a foot away?

"I'll miss you at the game tonight," he said, his face boyishly disappointed, his eyes full of questions.

"Will you?" She hated disappointing anyone and she had no answers to his questions or to the dilemma he'd brought to both of them.

"You know I will." He placed a hand on the brick behind her, effectively trapping her. "I wish…"

She shouldn't have asked but she did, just as she did a dozen things for Zak Ashford that made her pathetic. "What do you wish?"

"That things were different. I wish I'd been smarter and made better choices. This has messed us up, hasn't it?"

He had no idea. As clichéd as it sounded, she said, "You can't change the past. Doing the right things now is what matters."

"Yeah. At least, I *think* so. I've prayed about it a lot," He shifted, touched her hair. She tried not to enjoy his nearness, tried not to yearn.

Was it a sin to love him?

"Me, too."

"I told Pastor Parker about us."

"About us?" Alarmed, she pushed at his arm. There was no us. There couldn't be. "Stop it. You didn't! Zak, how could you?"

"I needed his advice."

"What did he say?"

"What could he say? My situation with Crystal is a gray area with no clear scriptural directive. He advised me to pray and follow my conscience." His mouth tilted a little then. "Darn thing is giving me fits."

She heard that.

"You shouldn't have said anything." And when he looked more lost and forlorn, she relented. "I'm not doing a very good job of staying away from you."

"Friends don't run away in hard times." He stroked her arm, found her fingers and squeezed. "I'd go crazy without you right now. I'm going crazy anyway, but when you come around I find my center, at least for a little while."

"Don't," she said. *Please don't make me love you any more than I already do. Don't put me in the middle. Don't make me feel used and guilty.*

Heedless of her inner battles, he gathered her into his arms and pressed her head to his shoulder. He smelled wonderful. Like clean sweat and cotton t-shirt and his simple brand of spiced shaving lotion. A torrent of emotion raced through her. If she could stop time and stay right here, she would.

"Hey, Zak," a voice interrupted.

Jilly and Zak jumped apart to find Brent staring curiously at them from the end of the house.

"Dude, we're ready to set up the cross bar. You coming?"

Looking every bit as guilty as she felt, Zak nodded. "Sure am." He glanced back at Jilly. "See you later. Okay?"

Numbly, she nodded and as he sauntered away, she leaned her head back against the hard brick and stared at the blazing yellow sun. Blood racing, face hot with embarrassment, she promised herself one more time to keep a friendly distance.

This time, she had to keep that promise.

Jilly didn't come to his game that night, and his pitching had been lousy. Coach had yanked him in the third inning, a humiliation he hadn't endured since college.

Jilly was his good-luck charm, his cheerleader, his go-to girl. And she hadn't been there.

She didn't come to the next two games, either. Matter of fact, he didn't see her all week and even though he'd called and texted her, she hadn't answered. Once, he'd talked to her mom, but Diane had behaved as if he had leprosy and hadn't even invited him in.

If he'd known talking to Pastor Parker would upset her, he wouldn't have. Particularly because the conversation hadn't helped at all. No matter how much he insisted to the contrary, the marriage, according to Pastor Parker, was real. There was no absolution for stupidity, even if the deed had been done on the cusp of adulthood ten years ago.

Other than the problem of Jilly, though, things were on the upswing. He'd worked up the nerve to call his parents who, though stunned, had offered support, something he'd need more than ever if Jilly abandoned him. The kids had actually gone through a week without a major incident and had surprised him this morning when he'd come in from work with a spotless house, made beds and breakfast on the table. Granted, the breakfast was a bowl of raisin bran and a glass of apple juice, but they'd been proud of themselves. He'd been proud, too. He'd texted Jilly with the story, convinced she'd be as pleased as he was. She hadn't replied to that text, either.

He was starting to get the message in big red letters.

Tired and eager for a few hours' sleep, he first headed down the hall to check on Crystal. Annie said she'd had a rough night.

Bracing himself for the inevitable stab of pity, he found Jake at Crystal's bedside and Bella sitting on the clean covers at her mother's hip. Brandon was nowhere around, an occurrence that made Zak's shoulders tense. Trust would be a while in coming.

Other than the quiet ticking of the IV pump, now a permanent fixture in the house, the room was hushed. Annie was there to reposition her patient and take care of basic needs, but they'd come to a point of waiting.

Waiting for a person to die was a horrible endeavor.

Crystal moaned. Zak glanced at Annie, wondering if he should take Jake and Bella outside. More and more he and

Annie kept them away from her room, kept them quiet, tip-toed around the house to let their mother rest. She hadn't been out of bed for more than a week and he doubted she ever would again.

A sharp pang gripped a spot somewhere in his heart he'd reserved for this woman. He must have cared about her at one time, although all he could remember was her neediness.

Some things never changed, even though the current need was one she could not control.

God help her. Help us all.

"Zak." The word came with such softness he had to move closer to the bed.

"Right here," he said.

Her stick-thin arms snaked out from beneath the covers. With one hand she touched Jake and then Bella. With the other hand she clawed the air toward Zak. He enfolded her skeleton fingers, found them as bloodlessly cold as their bluish color indicated.

Her eyes fell shut and she said nothing else for a while. A soft gurgle issued from the back of her throat and her breathing was erratic. Zak found himself counting each respiration, watching the rise and fall of her birdlike chest. Breathe, breathe, breathe. Silence. Breathe again.

Profound sadness weighed him down. He looked to Annie again, wondering if Jake and Bella belonged here. "The kids?"

By now, Bella had curled close to Crystal and lay very still, watching her mother's face with wide blue eyes. Jake stood at the bedside, sucking his thumb, something Zak wasn't seeing that much anymore.

Annie, a stethoscope dangling over the Faith Hospice logo, put her hands on the boy's shoulders. "Jakey, how about a popsicle?"

Bella sat up, dog-eared ponytails askew. "I posicle."

With her gentle kindness, Annie lifted Bella to her hip and steered Jake through the doorway. "We'll be in the kitchen if you need us."

Zak nodded, aware that Annie was giving him time alone with his dying wife. A fist gripped his gut. What was he supposed to feel other than helpless and alone? Pity, perhaps, for he had plenty of that.

"Zak." This time Crystal's voice was barely a rasp. "Don't let them forget me."

The request stabbed him full in the chest.

"I won't," he managed around a lump of pity thick enough to choke him.

It bothered him not to be able to give her something better than his pity. How cruel and ugly that life had robbed her of parents and siblings, of loved ones to share her passing. Someone other than a man she'd barely known should be here for her. Crystal deserved to be loved, to be mourned by more than three children hardly old enough to understand what was happening.

"We took pictures, remember?" When she'd first arrived, when she'd been strong enough to walk outside and sit on the porch. When she'd watched TV and sat at the table. The day she'd drawn pictures with her children, and another when they'd read to her and her to them. Even though the days had been short and her fatigue short-circuited many activities, they'd taken pictures. Jilly's idea. She'd recognized the need when he hadn't.

Crystal's lips curved, although a permanent pinch of pain tortured her face. A bead of moisture formed in the corner of one eye. Her fingers convulsed in his.

"Are you in pain?" he asked.

"Pray."

He wasn't much of one to pray out loud, but he did

anyway. He could do that much for her. He prayed for her pain, for Jake, and Brandon, and Bella. He prayed for wisdom to care for them.

"Most of all, Father," he murmured, aware of the involuntary flexing and unflexing of her fingers against his. "Give Crystal peace and comfort. No worries anymore. No fear. No pain. Trust in You."

Her hand went limp and he jerked his eyes open, heart pounding. Even though he'd seen death, he didn't want to see this one.

She looked relaxed, blessedly asleep. For a second, he thought she was gone, but then she pulled in a shudder of air. Even a few minutes escape from the ravaging pain and drugged haze was a mercy for her now.

Zak folded her hand beneath the sheet and sat down in the chair next to the bed. He wished Jilly was here. She'd know what to do.

He fished in his pants pocket for his cell to tap out a text but changed his mind. Jilly was at work. He'd promised himself not to burden her, not to ask, not now when she'd turned her back. He pocketed the phone and leaned forward to rest his elbows on his knees and his forehead on his laced hands.

His own struggles lost their power in the wake of Crystal's condition.

Fatigue of working a twenty-four-hour shift with little downtime caught up with him. He tilted back against the easy chair. If he could close his eyes for a few minutes, he'd be okay.

The door opened to admit Annie. With her quiet compassion, she trailed fingertips over his shoulder before moving to Crystal's side. "Go get some sleep."

Grateful, Zak unwound himself from the chair and stumbled down the hall to his bedroom where he fell, fully dressed, onto the navy coverlet. The house was eerily quiet and before sleep claimed him, he wondered where the children were.

Jilly had both hands on a wiggling Jack Russell terrier when her cell phone rang. She ignored the phone in favor of controlling the frightened dog who took exception to Dr. Bowman removing broken glass from his paw.

"Got it," the vet exclaimed, holding up an inch sliver pinched in a forceps.

Jilly relaxed her hands enough to stroke and soothe the quivering animal. "Good boy, Zero. You're okay now."

"I can take over," he said, "if you want to check your messages."

Jilly blushed, the hated heat flooding her face. "Sorry, I should have turned it off, but with my neighbor so sick…"

"You don't have to explain. Go ahead." He hitched his chin toward the door. "Tell Mrs. Watkins to come on back. Zero will be happy to see her."

Jilly did as he asked and then keyed in the password to her voice mail. The first message was Annie with an update on Crystal. The news was, as she expected, not good. The second was from her mother. Brandon, Jake and Bella were with her. Crystal was, as Mom put it, "bad."

Her heart hurt for the three little kids whose mother wouldn't see them grow up. She ached for Zak, knowing how responsible he felt.

The phone rang again. This time she answered.

"Jilly?" Zak's voice broke over the line and she knew before he said the words.

Crystal was dead.

Chapter Fifteen

Later that evening, Zak wandered the length of his house, listened to the hushed voices of the good and decent people of Redemption. Armed with compassion and casseroles, they came. Colleagues from the fire department. Church friends. Baseball players and their wives.

The smell of freshly fried chicken, normally a favorite, overwhelmed him. He headed out the back door, across the yard to the play set he'd purchased for the three children who now belonged to him forever.

What was he going to do with three kids? Three grieving, stunned children whose only anchor was no more.

He heard the back door open, the sound of voices issuing out and then going silent again with the door's closing. Too full of sorrow and fear, he didn't turn around until a familiar hand touched his back.

Jilly.

She didn't say a word. She simply rested a hand against him, a comfort and a friend who knew without asking what he needed most.

"What am I going to do with three kids?" He asked the question again, this time aloud.

"What you've already been doing." She stepped around

in front of him, still in work scrubs. "Did you get any sleep at all?"

He couldn't fool Jilly. "No."

He'd barely closed his eyes when Annie had tapped on his bedroom door. He'd bolted upright, knowing by the look on her face.

"She's gone," Annie had said.

"But I just walked out," he'd answered stupidly, as though arguing the matter would change it. Then the self-reproach came. "I should have been with her. I should have stayed."

"No." Annie had put her nurse's hand on his shoulder. "She was waiting for you to leave."

He'd looked at her, uncomprehending.

"I see it all the time. Patients say their peace and then once their loved ones leave the room, they let go. It's almost as if she was sparing you and her children."

"Maybe she was."

"I'll take care of all the details, but I thought you'd want to tell the children. They're across the street with Diane."

"You knew this was coming."

"I suspected today or tomorrow at the latest."

He'd nodded, a punch-drunk prize fighter, and stumbled across the street to Jilly's house. At the time, Jilly hadn't been home.

But she was here now.

"Thanks for coming. I thought…" He let the words go. He'd thought she was through with him. That she'd abandoned him. But she was here now, and that's all that mattered.

She slid her hand into his. He clung to her, a life raft in an uncharted sea.

"The kids," he said.

"With Mom and Amber. They're all right. Only Brandon truly understands."

"I'm afraid for him. What if he starts up again?"

"You'll be there."

But would *she?*

Now was not the time to ask, and in reality, he had no heart to give at the moment. He'd expected release with Crystal's death. All he felt was sad.

In Jilly's view, a funeral service was no place for children. Yet, Bella, Jake and Brandon sat like starched dolls in the front row next to Zak. Jake cried and sucked his thumb. Brandon stared off into space, rigid and distant. Bella kept wiggling down from the pew to pluck a flower from the blue casket, a sight that wrung the heart right out of Jilly.

"I'm going up there with Zak," she whispered to her mother. From the back of the church, she could see the sad little family. They needed her.

Even though Mom didn't look happy, she said nothing, and Jilly clasped her white clutch in both hands and made her way to the front, her heels making soft tap-taps on the thin carpet. Let people talk. She didn't care. Not today.

The expression on Zak's face bolstered her determination. Desperation and grief. Whether he knew it or not, Zak had cared about Crystal. Maybe he'd never loved her, but he had cared.

"Thanks," he murmured when she swept Bella away from the casket and onto her lap, bringing along a carnation for the toddler to play with. Crystal wouldn't mind.

The funeral proceeded. Pastor Parker officiated the brief service. No one in the community knew Crystal, but they knew Zak, and they had come for him.

Afterward, the attendees filed out with Zak, Jilly and the children coming last to complete the southern ritual of greeting the bereaved as the casket was rolled out to the hearse.

Jilly held Bella and watched, eyes burning as Jake and Brandon shook hands like little men and acknowledged hugs from strangers. Zak, one hand firmly on each boy, murmured his gratitude over and over again.

"So nice of you to help out, honey," one woman said to Jilly. "Zak's fortunate to have you right next door anytime he needs a sitter."

Even though the woman meant nothing by it, the statement stung. Jilly didn't reply. She couldn't. Her sister's words rang in her ears. Now that Zak was guardian to three children, he'd expect her to babysit while he played ball or worked or hung out with friends. He'd take advantage because she'd always let him. He'd need her more than ever.

But being needed was no longer enough.

She shook off the selfish thoughts. Today, three children mourned their mother. Tomorrow was soon enough to let go of her infatuation with Zak Ashford.

Every bone in Zak's body ached as if he'd fought fire for forty-eight hours and rescued a dozen victims single-handedly. He hadn't been this tired the weekend he'd played five back-to-back ball games after a shift at the fire station.

Now that the excruciatingly long day was over and night had come, he and the children watched a mindless television show, too numb for anything else. Jake and Brandon snuggled close to his sides, feet propped on the ottoman next to his. Bella lay across his belly, her head against his chest. In pajamas and smelling of soap and toothpaste, they were a stack of humanity drawing comfort from each other. He could feel all three children breathing and thought back to Crystal's last moments.

She'd been at peace. He was thankful for that.

The TV show ended but no one moved.

"Time for bed," he said, hoisting Bella into his arms to stand.

The boys trudged in front of him, down the hall. Jake glanced at the closed door of Crystal's room.

"I kiss Mama night-night," Bella said and stretched toward the room.

"She's not here anymore." Brandon's sharp tone brought a look from Zak. Then he saw the glisten of tears and knew how hard the boy was trying to hang on.

"I want Mama," Bella insisted.

How did he explain to a three-year-old that her mother was never coming back? Even though he and Pastor Parker had counseled with all three, Bella was too young to understand death as permanent.

He should have asked Jilly to stay longer. She would know what to do.

In over his head, he simply said, "We can't."

Somehow they got through the routine of bedtime. He listened to prayers, tucked them in and said goodnight.

After turning off the light, he pulled the door shut and headed toward his own bed, but as he passed the former sick room, he stepped inside. Someone—Annie, he supposed—had returned the space to its previous appearance. Gone were the machines, the medications, the random trappings needed for the sick and dying. The scent of cleaners and furniture polish replaced the smells of sickness. A plug-in air freshener shot a flowery fragrance through the air.

Friends were gold.

Yet, he wondered if he could ever look at this room the same way again.

Quietly closing the door behind him, he went to the kitchen where he considered but decided against a snack.

The Cubs were playing tonight but he didn't even have the heart for baseball.

What was he going to do with three grieving kids? How would he cope? How would they?

In his bedroom, he slipped beneath the sheet and clicked off the lamp to lay with hands behind his head, staring into the darkness. Stillness hovered over the house.

Jake came first. Zak heard the soft footfalls and saw the small shadow, silhouetted by the hall night-light.

"Can I sleep with you?" the whisperer asked.

Zak simply scooted over and tugged the child down next to him. Before he had time to adjust the sheet, the other two came.

"Bella's scared," Brandon said and Zak heard the bravado.

Zak patted the opposite side of bed. "Climb in. Both of you."

Brandon didn't argue and in seconds the four of them were crowded into Zak's California king. After a bit of adjustment, everyone settled. Zak closed his eyes. Maybe now he could sleep.

"Zak."

His eyes flew open. "What, Brandon?"

"What's it like to die?"

His pulse jumped. Considering he'd never died before, he was no expert. "Are you asking about your mother?"

"I guess." The child's voice was painfully small and wounded.

"You remember how much pain she was in?"

The darkness around them ached. "Yeah."

"She doesn't hurt anymore. She's at peace."

"Is she in heaven with Jesus? Pastor said she was."

Zak swallowed, feeling inadequate while aware he was all they had. "Yes."

Beside him Jake squirmed and the sound of thumb sucking ceased. "Will we die, too?"

"Not for a long, long time, Jakey. Most people don't get as sick as your mother did. Most of us live to be very old."

"Like Popbottle Jones?"

Zak smiled down at the shadow child. "Even older."

"Wow, that's really old." Jake wiggled again, turning his face toward Zak's although they could barely see each other. "Can I have a junk yard, too, and make bicycles for kids?"

A six-year-old was a small, innocent creature. "If that's what you want when you grow up."

"Not me," Brandon said from his spot under Zak's right arm. "I want to be a fireman and put out fires and keep people safe."

Zak hugged the boy's thin shoulders, touched and relieved. A man who battled fires wouldn't go around setting them. "You'll make a great firefighter someday."

"What do you want to be when you grow up, Zak?" asked Jake.

"He's already grown up, stupid."

"Hey." Zak squeezed Brandon's shoulder. "No name calling. When I was your age, I wanted to be a baseball player."

"You are."

"He means a major leaguer," Brandon said and Zak heard him bite off the "stupid" word. "He wants to pitch for, like, the Yankees or somebody famous."

"You can be a major if you want to." Jake wiggled, restless in the crowded bed. "You're the best pitcher in the whole world."

Heaviness pushed on Zak's chest like a heart attack. "Don't think I'll make it now, Jakey, but thanks for the compliment."

The room was silent for a while and he hoped the boys

had fallen asleep the way Bella had. She'd zoned out the minute he'd helped her onto the bed.

He closed his eyes, praying for sleep. Accustomed to sleeping alone, he felt crowded by the three extra bodies, their warmth heating up the temperature of the room. He also felt comforted and right somehow to have the trio snuggled next to him.

Jake muttered something and Zak realized he was asleep. He wished sleep would come for him, but when it didn't, he thought and prayed. He thought about the future, about how he would raise three motherless children alone. And that thought brought Jilly to mind.

What would he do if she turned her back on them? She had carried them through this difficult day, knowing instinctively what was needed and doing it without a word from him. Would she continue, now that the storm of dying and death had passed?

"I love her, Lord," he murmured.

She liked the kids, but being a parent was far more challenging than being a friendly neighbor. Was he fair to drag her into this? Was it even right for him to be longing for his neighbor on the day he'd buried his lawful wife?

Probably not.

"Why won't you go? The kids miss you. I miss you. Come on, Jilly, throw me a bone." Zak slapped an agitated hand on the hood of Jilly's car. He'd cornered her in the driveway as soon as she'd gotten home from work. "It's a carnival, for crying out loud. You love carnivals."

Yes, she did and she also loved him, the big lug. A week since Crystal's funeral and she was miserable.

"I see the kids." Because, like the doormat she was, she rushed over to his house on his workdays to stay with them until the sitter arrived and until she left for the clinic. The three were resilient, as kids tend to be, but she ached for their loss, and she would be there for them, regardless of her family's dire warnings.

Last night, Amber had suggested she offer to marry Zak, convinced he wouldn't turn her down because, after all, he'd be getting a mother for those pitiful children. The way her sister had talked, such a bargain was Jilly's only hope of ever finding a husband.

Right now, she thought her sister may have been right. Even if she wasn't, how could Jilly know for sure if Zak loved her for herself or because he desperately needed help with his new and often-challenging family?

She couldn't.

With a harangued sigh, she opened the back car door and reached for the grocery bags.

Zak took them from her. "What's wrong with you? Ever since the funeral, you've been weird. Did I do something I shouldn't have?"

Besides take me for granted? "I *feel* weird."

He paused at the back door, bags easily balanced in his long arms. "You do? Why? About what?"

She hadn't intended to tell him. "You know why."

He rolled his eyes toward the sky. "No, I don't. I'm a guy, remember? We don't get it most of the time."

The paper grocery bags crinkled as she tried to grab them from his hands. "I can carry these."

"So can I." He shouldered her out of the way. "Why do you feel weird? Why are you *acting* weird?"

She gave the door a yank, letting him pass into the cool house. July had come and true to form, Mother Nature had turned up the heat. July, with its celebrations and fireworks and carnivals. She prayed the distractions would be good for the kids.

The two rat terriers came charging in to dance around

her feet. She waded past them, remotely aware of their nails tapping, tongues lolling and tails in a whirlwind of wiggles. Normally, she reveled in their excitement. Today, she stepped around them, distracted by Zak's persistence.

He set the two bags on the kitchen table and turned. She bumped into him. He caught her shoulders. "What's happened to us, Jilly? Is it the kids? Are they too much for you?"

"No! Don't think that." Her sister's words buzzed in her brain. "None of this is their fault. It's just that I feel guilty and," she shrugged, embarrassed, "kind of awkward when I'm with you."

"Guilty of what? Crystal's gone."

"That's the problem! It's as if I'd wanted her to die so I could be with you."

"That's ridiculous. No one wanted her to die." As if her words had just made sense, Zak stilled, eyes narrowed. "Are you trying to say you want to be with me? As in, you might love me?"

"No." She twisted her head to one side, unable to face him. "Yes."

He pulled her gently around, hugging her to him as he tilted her face to his. "Love is not wrong, Jilly."

A tear leaked from the corner of her eye. "I can't help how I feel."

"Hey, don't cry." Hands raised, Zak stepped back, and Jilly felt the loss clear to the rubber soles of her white shoes.

Jilly slapped away the tears, stubbornly jutting her chin. "I'm not crying. I just can't go anywhere with you right now. I need some…time."

With a sigh, he said, "The kids will be disappointed."

She jabbed a finger at him. It trembled, betraying her, "Don't put that on me."

Both his palms shot higher in surrender. "Just saying. You've helped them a lot. Me, too."

Need. It was always about need.

"Please go." *Go, before I make a bigger fool of myself.*

Eyes green as spring gave her a long, bewildered stare. To escape his scrutiny, Jilly crouched to her dogs, rubbing comfort from the squirming pair. She knew he didn't understand. Neither did she.

Zak moved, tennis shoes scraping the tile, and then he was gone, leaving her to second-guess her behavior. What was wrong with her? For years, she'd wanted Zak to return her feelings. Now that he was trying to do exactly that, she pushed him away. He used to be her best friend, the guy she could talk to about anything.

Since Crystal's death, she'd been incredibly confused. About her feelings. About him. About everything. Because the truth was, she believed her sisters. Zak didn't love her. He needed her.

And she was selfish enough to want more.

Chapter Sixteen

Zak played in a tournament that weekend. Jilly refused to come, so he'd enlisted his teammate's wife to keep an eye on the rug rats during the games.

Sweat rolled down the sides of his face. He gulped another cup of Gatorade to keep the electrolytes balanced and the body running at full steam. Steam being the operative word in this heat. Near the corner of the dugout, Zak found enough shade to cool off while his teammates batted.

"What's the deal with Jilly?" Hunter Case asked, tossing his glove on the metal bench next to Zak. His red hair looked like fire beneath the blazing sun. "She never comes to the games anymore."

Zak shrugged his pitching arm into a jacket sleeve and leaned back to stretch his long legs out in front. "I asked the same question."

"What did she say?"

"She feels weird being seen with me."

"What does that mean?"

Zak shrugged. "Welcome to the 'I have no idea' club."

"Women are a mystery."

A bat cracked against the hard ball. All heads turned to watch, including Zak's. A ground ball single to right field.

When the brief celebration ended, he said, "I'm in love with her, Hunter."

"Bro, that is no surprise to this old lawyer." Dirt stuck to the sweat under Hunter's chin, a far cry from his normal suave attorney look. "You two have been crazy about each other for as long as I can remember."

"We have?"

Hunter took off his cap, wiped sweat and readjusted the head gear with a chuckle. "I hope I never have to call you as a witness. You're not very observant. Wake up, chump. Jilly Fairmont's a catch, and she's never looked at any guy since you moved to town."

"How do you know?"

Hunter popped his chest with two fingertips. "'Cause I asked her out, along with a couple other guys on this team, and she said no to all of us." When Zak bristled, Hunter dipped to one side, grinning. "Don't hit me. That was years ago. According to my bar scores, I'm a smart man. I figured out fast why she turned me down."

Zak swallowed. Jilly had been in love with him for years? How could he have been so blind? "That long?"

"Yes, that long." Hunter shook his head, grinning in mock pity.

"Why didn't you say something?"

"Wasn't my place to nose into your love life."

"Then, why now?"

"Because now you need a shove. And we need a pitcher with his head in the game. Think about it, Ash. When Crystal arrived on the scene, Jilly was pushed out."

"I didn't know." He stared down at the dust collected on his black Nike cleats. Jilly hadn't said a word. She'd encouraged him to care for Crystal and when he'd finally realized it was Jilly he loved, she'd rejected him. "Can't I plead ignorance?"

"Woman logic doesn't work that way. She loved you. You betrayed her by having a wife. Yet, who trooped right in and helped out with Crystal and her kids? Who was there when you needed a hand, showing her love in a thousand ways?"

Zak squirmed like a guilty man on the witness stand. "Jilly."

"Exactly what did you do to show yours?"

"Kissed her? Told her I love her?" Yeah, he'd done that. She should know.

"Dude, what am I going to do with you? Think about it. A man suddenly declares his love and kisses a woman after she discovers he's married and has a houseful of kids to look after. What kind of message does that send?"

The light started to dawn. Hunter Case must be a force in the courtroom. "She doesn't believe me."

"Nope."

"She thinks I'm using her."

"Aren't you?"

Someone called Hunter's name. "Case, you're in the on-deck circle."

Zak wagged his head, vaguely aware of an ant crawling up one sock. "I'm an idiot."

"The verdict is in." Hunter rose and slapped Zak on the shoulder. "Guilty."

"Okay, kids, here's the deal." Zak sat on the back step in a huddle with Brandon, Jake and Bella. Three sets of eyes stared at him. "We miss Jilly, right?"

Three heads bobbed.

"We want her to come over more, right?" He wanted a lot more than that, but it was a good place to begin.

"Yeah." Tilted forward in earnest conversation, arms

on his knees, Brandon imitated Zak's posture. "Is she your girlfriend?"

Nothing like getting to the heart of the matter. "I want her to be. Would that be a problem for you guys?"

"Nope," Jake said. "She has rabbits. And she's real nice."

"Wabbits," Bella parroted, looking around as if a bunny would hop over at any moment.

"What about you, Brandon? How do you feel about Jilly and me, together?"

A frown wrinkled Brandon's brow. Zak could tell something important was going on behind those intelligent brown eyes.

"I think you should marry her. We need a new mom. I think Jilly would be good at mom stuff."

Zak's chest tightened. The kid could slay him sometimes. "Marriage might be jumping the gun seeing as how she won't even go to a movie with me."

"Oh." Brandon's frown deepened. "Doesn't she love you anymore?"

What was this kid? A new Dr. Phil in the making? "I think she does, but I think I may have hurt her feelings."

"You have to say sorry. That's what you told us. When you hurt somebody's feelings, you say sorry."

Zak hid a grin at Jake's serious reprimand. "Agreed, but I need your help. Okay? The four of us, working together, can get Jilly back."

"What do we do? Give her presents?" Jakey asked. "I'll give her my red Hot Wheel."

Touched by the boy's willingness to sacrifice his favorite car, Zak patted his head. "That's nice of you, Jake, but I have a different idea. We'll show her we love her."

"How?" Jake's face twisted in puzzlement.

"Do stuff for her. Right, Zak?"

"Right, Brandon. But we're a family now. We do this together or not at all. Are you in?" He held out a hand.

Each child in turn slapped a palm atop his. "We're in."

Jilly awoke to a text message chime on her cell phone and a hotlink to a song. Curious, she followed the link and heard, "Miss You Like Crazy."

"Nice start to the day," she said to the pair of dogs sitting at the end of her bed, ears erect.

He missed her. He needed her. Been there, done that and had the doormat T-shirt to prove it.

A few minutes later, the doorbell chimed. Mugsy and Satchmo beat a path to the living room. Mother was already there, tying the sash of her terry-cloth robe. "Who in the world at this time of morning?"

When she opened the door, an envelope tumbled to the threshold. Jilly saw her name scrawled in childish letters. From the corner of one eye, Jilly spotted two small figures pounding a retreat toward Zak's house. Brandon and Jake?

What was going on this morning? "I think that's for me."

With her mother watching, eyes wide with curiosity, Jilly opened the envelope. Inside was a paper filled with colorful hearts, drawn by childish hands. Inside each heart was her name. Then in Zak's scrawl, "You're in my heart all day, every day and forever. Love, Zak."

When Mom stretched her neck to see, Jilly clasped the card to her chest. She was in his heart? For real? Her stomach jittered.

"Is that from Zak?"

"Mmm," she answered and with a smile wide enough to crack her face, Jilly headed to her room and got ready for work.

Three hours later, the flowers arrived at Dr. Bowman's clinic. Roses. Lots and lots of roses. Jeri Burdine, the re-

ceptionist and office manager, hollered for Jilly to get her
cute self up front.

"Must be from your fireman," Jeri declared, swinging
her head so the multicolored beads rattled together on her
braids. "Only a man buys that many roses. Girl, what did
he do that needs forgiving?"

Jilly fought the battle of the blush and lost when she
read Zak's name scrawled beneath the words, "You're more
beautiful than all the roses in the world. Beautiful to the
soul. I miss you."

A chip of ice melted in one corner of her heart. What
was he doing? Wooing her? Because if he was, it might be
working.

Throughout the day, sweet text messages bombarded
her phone until she turned it off. Dr. Bowman was an easy
boss. She didn't want to take advantage.

But she was starting to feel...special.

When she arrived home that evening, her shaggy lawn
had been mowed, the flower beds trimmed and cleaned. A
note stuck to the handle of her cranky old mower. "Your
mower looked tired. I used mine. The kids did the weed-
ing. They love you. Me, too. Zak."

She went to bed that night with a smile on her face and
a prayer on her lips. And a single pink rose clutched close
to her nose.

History repeated itself the next day. Sweet, silly, tender
notes on the door and stuck beneath the wipers on her car.
A bag of her favorite candy, a bouquet of Shasta daisies and
an invitation to dinner, all delivered by two grinning boys
who made the hand-offs and then thundered away, giggling.

She adored those little boys. But, oh, that man. That in-
credible man with the floppy smile and the greenest eyes
and the biggest heart. Oh, that man.

What was he doing to her?

"Zak must be on a four day," Jilly told Annie when they met for lunch on the third day of over-the-top attention. Inside the Sugar Shack, the scent of grilled burgers mingled with the sweet rolls and doughnuts that made the establishment popular. "He's probably bored."

"Give the boy a break, Jilly." Annie fluffed a paper napkin onto her lap.

"Do you think he really means it?"

"What a silly question. Why else would he send flowers every day and wash your car in the middle of the night and send all those adorable notes?"

Jilly toyed with the crust on her chicken salad sandwich. "Because of the kids. He needs help. I'm there."

"Is that what you believe? Truly?"

Jilly nodded, miserable with hope that she was wrong. "Look at me, Annie, and be honest. We've been friends for a long time. I am not beautiful, no matter what Zak's notes say. I'm a freckled redhead who blushes about everything, the kind people joke about. Half the time, my face is the color of that tomato."

"You're a beautiful woman, freckles and all. Your hair is gorgeous, the kind women pay money for at the Curl Up and Dye Salon." Annie placed a consoling hand on Jilly's. "Somewhere you've gotten the idea you aren't pretty, but I don't see it and Zak doesn't, either. Honey, Zak thinks you're the prettiest woman on the planet. Can't you understand that? I can. Sloan can."

"I wish I could. But it's not just the looks thing." Although that played a big part, Zak had never seemed to mind her freckles. In fact, he'd kissed them. Funny how she'd forgotten that and the way he'd called the ugly brown spots angel kisses.

"Then what is the problem?" Annie leaned back in the wooden chair and lifted her tea glass.

"Guilt."

She set the tea glass down. "What did you do?"

"Nothing! Annie, you know me better than that. Zak is married. I would never…"

Annie held up a hand. "Then why the guilt?"

Jilly blinked. If her best girlfriend didn't understand who would? "He's married."

"Was. And the circumstances were beyond strange."

"Which makes me even worse. I'm like a vulture or something, chasing after a man who barely knew his wife, a wife who recently passed away. People will gossip."

Annie took a bite of her salad, chewed and swallowed. "Have you talked to Zak about this?"

"Yes." The waitress came by, refilled teas and hurried away again. As usual, the Sugar Shack was hopping busy, the clatter of dishes, the rise of conversation and laughter, the call of "order up." She and Annie could talk about anything in this building and not be overheard.

"Then you know full well the circumstances of that marriage," Annie said. "You also know Zak sacrificed hugely to do the right thing for Crystal and her children, even when they were not his responsibility. Not many men would do that."

"He's a good man." The best. Good and kind and generous and funny.

"Crystal told me herself they were never a love match. Zak married her out of sympathy because, as you said, he's a good guy with a big heart." Annie pointed her fork. "Not, mind you, that I don't think he was out of his mind stupid to do such a thing, but if you remember, I've been on the other side of that coin. I understand where Crystal was coming from. I get why they both did what they did."

Jilly opened her mouth to speak and then closed it again. She knew Annie and Sloan's story, but she'd missed the parallels until this moment. Run out of town by Annie's father, Sloan had unknowingly left Annie alone and pregnant. She'd married another man to cover her humiliation and give her son a name, a decision that had proved disastrous. Years had passed before Sloan returned to Redemption, the truth came out and the couple reunited. They were happy now, but they'd traveled a long road to claim that happiness.

"I guess you do understand."

"I do. And like my feelings for my first husband, Zak never loved Crystal. He loves you just as I always loved Sloan. So wake up and embrace the moment. Both of you have done all you can to properly handle a bizarre situation. When adversity came, Zak stood up and did the manly thing. You could take a lesson from him."

Annie's blunt talk stunned Jilly into realization. Zak had been the one bearing the heaviest load. Not her. He'd been the one to make difficult choices that had affected the rest of his life. Not her. Sure, she'd helped him out now and then, but all along, she'd whined about herself. About what she wanted and couldn't have.

"Lord, forgive me. I thought I was being so pious." The word "self-righteous" was more like it.

"Does this mean you're going to give that man a chance?"

A smile started in Jilly's belly and spread upward to her chest and out onto her face, a face blushing hot pink. "He has a ball game tonight. I think I have a little surprise for him afterward."

"Are you going to tell him the truth once and for all?"

"That I love him like crazy? That I want to spend forever with him?" Life was too short to waste on bad choices and whining. Crystal's life and death had taught her that much. "Yes, I am."

Annie held up a hand. They slapped high fives.

Finally, Jilly felt free to embrace the relationship she'd always wanted and been afraid to believe in. Finally, she could tell Zak everything that was in her heart and accept the love he was offering.

She could hardly wait for tonight.

Zak knew something was up even before Coach Branson pointed out the scout sitting in the stands behind the catcher. He knew it from the heat in his midsection and the buzz in his bloodstream. He'd been scouted before in college, but he was a better pitcher now. Good enough for a small-town team to draw the attention of a big-league scout.

He was stoked. Right before the national anthem played over the scratchy CD player, his energy level jacked up another notch. Jilly strolled into the ballpark, gave him a cocky little two-fingered wave before climbing into the stands directly behind the scout.

Hunter Case saw the direction of his gaze and slapped him on the shoulder. "Must be your night, Ash."

"Man, I hope so."

"How's the arm?"

"Like a rocket." He rotated the shoulder, then punched a fist into his glove. "Jet-fueled and ready to fly."

"That's what I'm talking about, bro. Blow 'em away."

And he did.

After the game he wasn't even nervous when Coach introduced him to the scout from the Texas Rangers. As soon as the conversation ended, he searched the crowd for Jilly and found her sitting in her spot, watching him.

Sweaty, his teeth full of dirt from grinning, he loped through the gate, around the backstop, and clanged up the metal bleachers. When he reached her, Jilly stood, grinning, too.

"You were awesome." She hugged him.

He returned the embrace, his gloved hand patting awkwardly at her back before he stepped away. "I'm sweaty."

She tiptoed up and kissed his cheek. "I don't care."

They stood face to face, close as a whisper and Jilly wasn't backing away this time. His pulse jacked. Was his plan paying off? "You don't?"

"No, I don't. I don't care if you're sweaty or if you have three kids or if you've been married or even if you just pitched the most amazing ball game on the planet."

He must be dreaming. Life didn't get this good, did it? His heart, already going crazy with excitement over the scout's news, threatened to exit his chest. "I think I like the sound of this."

"I got your messages and the gifts and the flowers and the—" She laughed, eyes shining a message he'd waited a long time to hear. "Thank you."

"Does this mean you're talking to me again?"

"That's the plan."

Under the field lights, her freckles were gold dust, her hair copper, and if she didn't stop looking at him that way, he was going to kiss her like a madman right here in front of the crowd. Let 'em talk.

A handful of spectators filtered past, each one stopping to congratulate Zak on the good game. As much as he appreciated the fans, he was dying to tell Jilly his news.

"Can we go somewhere?" he asked when the well-wisher left. "I want to tell you something."

"I want to tell you something, too." She took his hand. "We'll take your truck. I caught a ride."

"On purpose?" he grinned.

"Yep." She bumped his side. "I wanted to ride with you."

This was his Jilly. Fun, lively, full of humor. What a relief. She was back. *Thank you, kids, for helping me out.*

He wished they'd come with him tonight, but Annie had asked them over to play with her kids for the evening.

"What if I refuse to take you home?" he teased. "I don't usually pick up strange women at ball games."

"Okay, then." She tossed her head and sniffed. "Someone else will come along."

If they hadn't been joking, his jealous monster would have kicked in. Hunter Case would jump at the chance to drive Jilly home. Which was not about to happen. Not tonight. Not ever if Zak had any say in the matter.

Beneath the bright lights of the ball field, they reached the parking lot and his truck. He tossed his glove inside and waited for Jilly to climb in. He felt good to be with her again, as if a weight had been lifted. He and Jilly, a great team.

The night couldn't get any better.

Cars exited the parking area, their lights fanning over the graveled road.

"Any place in particular you want to go?" he asked.

"Here is fine. As long as I'm with you."

He liked the sound of that. "So what did you want to tell me?"

She shook her head, a half smile around those gorgeous lips. "You first. I saw you talking to the guy with the radar gun, and now you're about to explode. What's happened?"

He tipped his head back against the headrest, gazed out at the pitcher's mound, a clear vision from his truck. The field was empty except for the coach and a groundskeeper who were picking up bases. He loved the look of a ballpark, the dirt infield, the green, green outfield. "I got some good news tonight."

"Tell me."

In the shadowy light, her face was turned up toward his. "Can I kiss you first?"

Her smile bloomed. She scooted beneath his arm and tilted her face. He kissed her and the world, already pretty good, centered.

"Aah, that's better," he said with a satisfied sigh, and feeling this good, he kissed her again, holding her close to soak in the pleasure that only Jilly brought. "You're back. Thank God you're back."

"To stay." She nuzzled his neck.

He caressed the side of her face. "For real?"

"Yes. Now, tell me your news."

As distracting as having Jilly next to him was, he couldn't get the scout's offer out of his mind. She'd be excited for him. His Jilly would do a Snoopy dance, jump and shout and tell him he would make it. She believed in him, always had. "The man with the radar gun was a pro scout."

Her surprised gasp pleased him. She sat back, staring. "What did he say? Was he there to look at you? He was, wasn't he?"

"He liked what he saw, Jilly." Zak rotated in the seat, too excited to sit still. "He's been following me for a while through Coach."

"Did you know this was going on?"

"Not until tonight. He's with the Rangers. I've been invited to travel with an all-star team with a shot at the minors before summer's over. Maybe even the majors."

"Zak." Her voice went quiet. "Oh, Zak. That's...incredible."

She moved slightly away from him and there was a stillness in her that hadn't been there before. Shock, he supposed. He felt that way, too. Bubbling with shock and energy, he was also scared and uncertain.

"I've waited so long for this and now...I don't know if I should do it."

"What are you talking about, silly?" She gave his arm a

push, although her voice retained the hushed quality. "This is your chance. You've waited your whole life for this. You have to go."

"I have responsibilities here. Three of them. They've only started to adjust. I'll have to leave them, probably with my parents which will mean another change, a new place, new people."

"God's given you a chance at your dream. He'll work this out, too."

"I want this, Jilly. I've wanted it forever."

"I know you do. And I want you to have it." She lifted those soft blue eyes to his and he wondered at the glisten of moisture. "The kids can stay with me when you travel. We'll make it work. We have to." A tear quivered on her bottom eyelashes.

"Why are you crying?"

"Happy tears." She wiped them away and smiled.

"Sure?" He tilted her chin, studied her wet, blue eyes.

"Very happy. For you."

"You'll be here when I get back?"

"Aren't I always?" He thought he heard her sniff. He'd never understand female tears. She cried when she was sad. She cried when she was happy.

Zak hooked an arm around her neck and pulled her back for another kiss. She tasted soft and salty, of tears and smiles. She was happy for him, right?

"See why I need you?" he asked. "You always say the right thing."

Chapter Seventeen

The memory of that kiss and a dozen others before he took her home lingered with Jilly. He'd been ecstatic. Out of his head with speculations and what-ifs. What if he made the majors? What if he could pitch in Yankee Stadium before the season ended? What if... He was like a little boy dreaming big dreams, although he was a man and his dreams were finally within reach.

So, she'd let him carry on, thrilled for him, although her heart had sunk lower than his ERA. He'd said he needed her.

After the onslaught of love from across the street, Jilly knew there was more than need involved, but for now, being needed had to be enough.

Zak had tasted of sweat and dirt and pure adrenaline, and even though her whole plan was shattered, Jilly knew she'd said all the right things. After everything he'd been through in the past few months, Zak deserved her support in this.

When he'd asked at her front door what she'd wanted to talk to him about, she'd avoided the whole truth when she tiptoed up and kissed him. "Thank you for the flowers and the notes."

He grinned, boyish and proud. "You deserve all those and more." Then before she could say another word, he'd whooped with joy and spun her around. "I'm getting my shot at the bigs!"

Yes, he was, and she was going to be a big girl about it.

"Jilly," Brandon asked, face a study in concentration. "Does this look good?"

The four of them, Brandon, Bella, Jake and Jilly, were decorating a batch of strawberry cupcakes for Zak. Her mother, whose silence spoke louder than all the reprovals in the world, manned the mixer and bowls of colored frosting.

"Very creative," Jilly said, eyeing the carefully applied strips of icing.

"It's supposed to be a baseball."

"I knew that."

Brandon giggled. "You did not."

It was good to hear the child laugh. She and Zak had worried most about him, but Brandon had handled well the news of Zak's long summer of travel, vowing to be the man of the house while Zak was away. His counseling sessions were changing him. So was life with a strong, stable man.

Tears crowded the back of her eyes. She spun away. "Back in a minute."

She rushed toward the bathroom. The ridiculous grief came at the oddest times, overwhelming her. Even though she put on a happy face for the kids, she didn't want Zak to leave.

But he would, and if he came home at all the rest of the summer, she'd be surprised.

The bathroom door opened and Mom stepped inside. Jilly braced herself for another round of I-told-you-sos.

"Don't, Mother. Please. I can't take the criticism today."

"He's not leaving forever."

"I'm not upset about that." At least, not completely. She knew he'd return. She also knew she was being ridiculous, but just once she wanted to be first place in Zak's life.

Diane rolled off a strip of tissue, folded the layers and handed them to Jilly. "Then what's wrong?"

"I wanted him to love me, Mom." She sniffed, dabbed at her leaky face. "Enough to stay. But you and Amber were right. He needs help with the kids. Out of that need he's using me, and I'm okay with that." She had to be. Having some of Zak was better than having none.

The admission cut right through her like a fierce north wind. Her lip trembled. She was such a baby.

Her mom closed the toilet lid and sat on the fluffy blue terry cover. "We were wrong about Zak's motives, honey."

"No, you were right. Isn't that pretty obvious at this point?"

"What's obvious is that Zak Ashford does love you, enough to trust you with these children, enough to believe you'll be waiting when he returns."

"You're the one who said he was using me. I'm a door-mat, remember?" She didn't completely believe that. Not anymore, but her family did.

"Your sisters and I should never have said those things. We were trying to protect you from getting hurt, but we hurt you instead."

"It's okay. I understand." She dabbed at her face with the tissue, not even caring that her face was red and blotchy.

"What you need to understand is that you're smart and lovely and kind. If Zak Ashford doesn't come back to you, he's a fool, and I'll tell him to his face."

"Mom." Jilly smiled at her mother's fiery attitude. "Don't get your blood pressure up."

Her mother tilted her head in concern. "You gonna be okay?"

Jilly nodded. "I'm tough. Like my mama."

"That's my girl. Now, let's go out there and fix those cupcakes, love on those children and get ready to give Zak a happy send-off. No more tears. Got it?"

Jilly wadded the tissue into a ball. "Got it."

Her dream could wait. Zak's couldn't.

Leaving was harder than he'd expected. With Bella wrapped around his lower leg and Jake hanging on his arm like a monkey, he waded toward his truck. Brandon tagged along, playing the big boy as he lugged Zak's gym bag filled with baseball gear.

"You'll be okay staying at my place?" he said to Jilly, who also carried a load. She and her mom had packed enough food to keep him alive on the Sahara.

"Of course, I will. You have cable."

He grinned. That was his Jilly. "I'll call you after every game."

"You better." She slipped a box onto the seat. He spotted more of his favorite cupcakes, each one with strange-colored icing and dotted with candy. The kids had been so proud of their first effort at baking, and he had to admit the cupcakes tasted better than they looked.

"Gotta go, kids. I have to join the team in OKC." His belly quivered. Today was the first day of the rest of his life.

He scooped Bella up, kissed her nose, tickled her enough to make her laugh and then put her on her feet.

"Give me a hug, boys."

Jake slung both arms around Zak's waist. "I love you, Dad. Promise you'll come back. Promise."

A thick lump threatened to choke off Zak's air supply. "I

promise. This is my house, buddy, and you make great cup-cakes." In a conspiratorial whisper, he added, "And there's that little thing about Jilly. I gotta come back."

This opportunity couldn't have come at a worse time. Leaving Jilly and the kids was ripping his guts out.

He hugged Brandon and then turned to Jilly. A dozen emotions hit him, like fireworks inside. "I don't know how to tell you how grateful I am for what you're doing."

"I don't want gratitude."

He moved closer, ran his hands up her soft, freckled arms, regret and worry tugging at him. Now that she was ready to move forward, he was leaving her behind. "What do *you* want?"

"Tickets to a major league game. What else?"

He laughed and so did she. The silliness broke the awful pall threatening to overtake the group. He hugged her and when she lifted her chin, he kissed her, wishing he could spend the next hour sharing his heart, kissing her, making her laugh. "I'm gonna miss you."

"Same here." She stepped back and gave him a push toward the opened door of the truck. "Now, go. Knock 'em dead. Show 'em what you got."

"When I get back…you and me…" He couldn't get the words out. If he told her how much he loved her, he wasn't certain he could drive away. "Are you sure you'll be okay?"

This time she gave him a shove. "Go *on*. We'll be awe-some."

"You *are* awesome." He climbed up in the cab and started the engine. Four beautiful faces stared at him. Faces he loved. Faces he'd dream of and think of every waking moment. Faces with tears streaming down their cheeks.

He put the truck in reverse and slowly rolled out of the driveway.

He drove past the fire station, thankful for a fire chief

who believed in him enough to allow the leave of absence. If he failed at baseball, he'd still have a job he loved.

Three fellow firefighters manned the fire hose outside the station, washing the pumper truck. They'd subdued another grass fire last night. Brandon had been with Zak, a huge relief. The boy would be all right. Jilly promised to continue the firesetters prevention classes and she was pouring her heart and soul into nurturing his three charges.

Jilly. If a man could be in two places, he would be. He hadn't wanted to leave her. Not now. Not ever.

He slowed and honked his horn. The guys recognized him and waved, shouting, although he couldn't hear with his heart pounding in his ears.

He'd miss his job. He'd miss these guys and his church and this little town of Redemption that had embraced him with open arms.

Last night he'd slept little. Excitement mixed with dread had kept him awake. Would the kids be okay without him? Was he doing the right thing by leaving them behind this soon?

The fire station disappeared from sight as he turned the corner and headed through town. GI Jack and Popbottle Jones, trash bags hoisted over their shoulders, exited the alley behind Simmy John Case's hardware store. He gave them a honk and a salute, smiling at the two old characters who exemplified his adopted town.

Mowed grass smells filtered in through his air-conditioner vents. A city worker manicured Town Square, the pretty park in the center of town. Doc Bowman exited the Sugar Shack carrying a white bakery sack—the morning doughnut run for the employees at Jilly's workplace.

He hoped she could handle the stress of three kids and her job. He'd asked a lot of her, and experience had taught him how hard it was to be a parent. Hard but rewarding in ways he couldn't explain. After all the struggle against taking them as his own, he loved them with a fierce, protective love.

Would they be all right without him?

With an unexpected lump of nostalgia and regret, Zak aimed the truck toward the highway leading out of Redemption. He clicked on the radio and the CD player whirred into play mode. He must have left a disk in the slot by mistake.

Bella's favorite song swelled out from the speakers. She'd quickly picked up the tune and half the words, singing in her sweet baby voice, "When I wake up in the morning and lay my head to rest, I am blessed, I am blessed."

Bella had sang, "I am bwessed."

As he listened to the words, Bella's pert face was framed in his mind. Would she cry for him? Would she crawl in bed with Jilly tonight, afraid because he wasn't there to chase the monsters out from under her bed? He'd made a game of it, drawing laughter and confidence from the toddler who had wound herself around his heart. Daddy's little girl.

Up ahead, Redemption River glistened red and wavy beneath the hot July sun. He'd wanted to take Brandon and Jake fishing this summer. Maybe camping.

The truck tires bumped up onto Redemption River bridge, a quaint turn-of-the-century structure first built for the horse-and-buggy days. Zak slowed the truck, rolled down a window to breathe in the wet, fertile scent of the river.

Life was good here in Redemption. He was, as the song said, blessed. Blessed with a job he loved, with a woman who loved him even if she never said the words. He knew she loved him. Why else would she be at his house right now, holding down the fort while he pursued the brass ring of fame and fortune?

A check of the clock told him there was plenty of time for the trip to OKC. He pulled the truck to the side of the road, parked and got out to walk across the bridge. Traffic was slow in and out of the small town and today not another car was in sight. He stood at the stone wall of the bridge and gazed down at the gently flowing water.

Playing ball was all he'd ever wanted, wasn't it? He wasn't leaving forever. Yet, it felt that way.

The red water swirled below, red like Jilly's hair but nowhere near as beautiful. He imagined her face in that last moment as he'd driven away. She'd been crying and he wasn't dumb enough to believe those were tears of joy.

"Father, am I making the right choice?"

All his life, he'd wanted nothing more than a career in baseball, to see his name splashed on the sports page and watch highlights of his pitches on ESPN.

Now that the opportunity dangled in front of him, his for the taking, baseball didn't seem as important as before.

He bowed his head, listening to the quiet voice in the center of his being, the voice that wouldn't lead him astray. All he had to do was listen.

A slow awakening dawned, like a morning sun rising over the horizon. The soft gurgle of river below, the rustle of leaves in the willows, the scant ripple of breeze tickling his skin played around him, filling his senses, although the one true sense filled his spirit.

Baseball had paled, had been demoted by a trio of messy kids and a woman who rescued rabbits.

Suddenly, he knew with a clarity what had eluded him. He didn't want to go anywhere. Watching a young, once-vibrant woman die had taught him two valuable lessons: Life was short; choose carefully.

He rubbed his left arm, a habit of a lifetime, and asked

himself a question. Which would he rather hold? Jilly or a baseball?

Gaze fanning the river bank, the sand bars, the adjoining meadows, Zak took a long pull of summer air and a smile began to tickle his chest. Then his face. Until he laughed out loud.

He ran back to his truck, his future decided.

Jilly was determined not to mope. On a hot July day there was one easy way to avoid the blues.

"Everyone get your swim suit on."

"Are we going swimming?"

"Better than swimming. We're going to play in the sprinkler."

They bought it. With whoops of delight, the trio bolted for their rooms, Mugsy and Satchmo jingling along behind. By the time they were dressed and out the door, Jilly had found Zak's box of water toys and had hooked up the hose and sprinkler.

Even though her entire being felt lethargic and depressed, she pushed through the emotions for the sake of her charges. If she cried, the water would cover her tears.

"Aren't you gonna play, Jilly?" Jake had that worried look again.

"Sure am." She glanced down at her shorts and shirt. "These will dry." She turned the sprinkler on herself, gasped at the shot of icy water against hot skin, but laughed with the kids' squeals of excitement.

"Me next," Brandon yelled and ran through the arc, yelling with arms flailing in the air.

The others followed, running back and forth with childish abandon, the trauma of Zak's leaving taking a backseat to the moment of play.

Except for Jilly. Her heart hurt so badly that she wondered if this was what a heart attack felt like. More than that, she wondered where Zak was? Was he missing them yet? Probably not. His passion was baseball, not family. His focus was a future in the game he loved.

Although a man in every way, Zak was also an overgrown kid. His water toys proved that. She filled a couple of water guns and let the boys have at it. The war was on between Jake and Brandon, so she and Bella sat on the wet grass and let the sprinkler cycle around and around.

Jake came flying past yelling like a banshee with Brandon in hot pursuit, the dogs on his heels. "Save me. I'm out of ammo."

She laughed in spite of her depression. What great kids they'd become and how special in such a short time. All they'd needed was stability and love and a man named Zak.

The race circled around her, making tighter and tighter spins until Jake's feet slipped out from under him and he landed with a hard thud. Eyes wide, he sat up. Jilly held her breath, worried he would break into a howl. Instead, he giggled and scooted next to her, his drippy water smell clean and welcome.

Out of the blue, he asked, "Is Zak coming back?"

"Not today, but he will."

He picked at the grass stuck to his legs. "Mama went away and she didn't come back."

Jilly's stomach kerplopped. She slid an arm around Jake's waist. "Zak isn't sick like your mama. He'll come back."

Someday.

"What if he dies?"

"Everyone dies," Brandon said quietly. She hadn't realized he'd come to stand behind her.

"Zak is not going to die. Not for a long time." That was

a promise she shouldn't make, but today she would. "He's going to play baseball."

"Why can't he play here like always? I want him to be here."

They'd had this discussion. "So do I, Jakey, but sometimes a person gets a chance to do something special."

"Aren't we special?"

She closed her eyes, praying for help and trying to hold back the tears. Not special enough.

"Incredibly special. Just think, when Zak gets rich and famous, he can take you anywhere you want to go."

"I like it here."

"Me, too." Brandon pulled up a patch of grass, water dripping from his hair down onto his face. She assumed it was water and not tears. "I'm never leaving here. This is going to be my home forever."

"If Zak comes home," Jake said. "What if he doesn't? What if he forgets about us? What if he finds other kids to love? Where will we go?"

"Zak wouldn't do that," Brandon said, his face an angry scowl. "Never."

Oh, Zak, she thought, *was leaving as hard for you as it was for us? Or have you already put us on the back burner?*

Bella climbed up on her lap and clung, quiet. She'd need a nap soon.

Out on the street, cars puttered past and doors slammed. There, in the backyard, a hodgepodge family sat beneath a rotating sprinkler, mindless of the occasional spray, all of them a little too sad to play, all of them missing Zak.

"I'm gone less than an hour and you're already running up the water bill."

The familiar male voice had them all spinning toward the sound.

"Dad!" The two boys leaped from the grass, flinging

droplets and dirt from their heels in their haste toward the lanky man with the wide grin.

"Zak?" Jilly rose more slowly to set Bella on her feet. "Did you forget something?"

And do you know how hard it is going to be to watch you drive away again?

"Yep, sure did." The boys hit him at full speed. He caught them in a hug and dragged them forward as he advanced toward Jilly.

"What was it?"

He didn't answer for a moment. He kept coming, those long strides eating up the space, boys dangling from him like appendages, until they stood face to face. His eyes searched hers. "I almost forgot the most important thing. You."

Her pulse set up a racket. She must not have heard correctly with all the blood rushing in her ears. "Me?"

"You and my favorite rug rats. And my home and all the blessings I already have."

"What are you saying?"

"I'm not going with the all-star team. I'm not chasing a baseball career anymore."

"But it's your dream."

"Not anymore. You're my dream. You and these kids. It took leaving to understand that. I had to choose...and I choose you."

If she hadn't been standing in broad daylight soaking wet, she would have been certain she was hallucinating. He'd chosen her over baseball, over the dream he'd worked toward his entire life? "I don't know what to say."

"Say you're happy."

"I am."

"Say you love me."

"I do." As soon as the words left her mouth, he swooped

down like a giant eagle and snatched her against him for the sweetest kiss.

Her heart sighed. Zak was home.

Epilogue

Annie and Sloan offered the Wedding Garden, but Jilly and Zak opted for the unusual—a wedding held on the banks of Redemption River.

"So we can invite the whole town!" Jilly had said.

And that's exactly what they did. The ball team and guys from the fire station, people from church and work, family and friends from all over came that cloudy September afternoon to see Jilly Fairmont marry her best friend forever, Zak Ashford.

Waiting for his bride along the banks of the river, Zak embraced the history of the place, a river where Redemption's founder, Jonas Case had baptized converts, thousands had fished and swam, strolled and picnicked, and one man had returned from the dead. Redemption roots went deep.

He wanted to be part of that.

His brother, Stephen, gave him a wink as they stood stiff in their tuxedos with groomsmen Jake and Brandon. Zak's palms sweated, but he'd never been happier. Nervous but certain.

Bella came, escorted by Amber and Nicole, Jilly's sister bridesmaids. His little girl tossed rose petals with abandon and a hint of mischief that brought indulgent smiles and a few chuckles. Bella was a gift, one of the rewards Pastor Parker had spoken of. Doing the hard stuff had turned out better than he'd ever imagined.

Then Jilly appeared and his nerves melted away. His pulse, however, went crazy. She was the most beautiful sight he'd ever seen, a vision in a long, white gown with apricot banding. She'd warned him of the color addition chosen to flatter her skin and hair. He'd asked her to show off her freckles because he adored them, and the strapless gown did exactly that. She was ripe peaches and golden cream sprinkled with brown sugar. The delicious cherry on top was crowned with a garland of white and apricot roses.

Their eyes locked and he pulled her toward him, toward the place where she'd be his wife. His only true wife.

Suddenly, she was there and Pastor Parker began the service. Jilly took his hand and centered him, although his head buzzed and he couldn't think. But he could feel and he could see the smile on Jilly's glistening apricot lips and the love in her blue eyes.

When Pastor said the final words and Jilly moved into his arms, the song playing on the CD rotated around in his head. "I am blessed, I am blessed."

Amen and amen. He was a blessed man.

With the ceremony over, they wandered the river banks hand in hand, greeting guests and sharing cake from the Sugar Shack. Miriam and Hank Martinelli gazed on in pride at their three-tiered creation of white and apricot as two glowing pregnant ladies, Kitty and Cheyenne, dished up punch. The men, Sloan, Jace, Kade and Trace, gathered in a huddle with his firefighter and baseball buddies, although now and then, each man found his wife's gaze and smiled or winked. Romance was in the air.

Thunder rumbled in the distance.

"The two of you should get a move on," GI Jack said, a

flower in his shirt pocket in honor of the day, along with a handful of wedding mints. "Rain's coming in."

Jilly's mother, pretty in a pale green suit and heels, added encouragement. "The captain's firing up the truck. He said to tell you he was ready whenever you are."

Another rumble of thunder, this one closer, accented her words. Guests cast concerned eyes toward the gathering clouds. No storms on the horizon, only rain, though nothing could dampen the happiness of the day. After a full afternoon of partying, Zak was ready to be alone with his bride.

"Let's find the children first," Jilly said, already scanning the crowd.

"There." He tugged her hand, reveling at the feel of his ring on her finger, and together they bid the children goodbye—for three days. Three days of alone time with each other while Diane played grandmother, and he and Jilly played newlyweds.

The captain tooted the horn, the sound raucous. Everyone turned, surprised at the unusual wedding conveyance but smiling with the rightness of the choice.

It was all about choices. Crystal had taught him that. Choices, stacked together, make a life.

"Ready, Mrs. Ashford?"

Her face wrinkled in pleasure. "I love you so much."

With a laugh, Zak hoisted his glorious bride onto the top of the waiting fire truck and climbed up beside her, holding her secure as Captain Porter in full dress uniform pulled the gleaming red machine onto the highway. White streamers danced from the bumper, strings of cans rattled the concrete, and the siren began to wail the news.

Jilly and Zak waved to the crowd of smiling faces, and then to please himself as well as the onlookers, he drew his bride into his arms, thanking God he'd had the sense to make the right decision—not once but twice.

Home was not a plate to cross with a fastball. Home was where his heart was. Home was where God's plan had always wanted him to be. Home was contentment and love, a red-haired woman and a houseful of kids.

He kissed her then and knew her joy matched his as the truck rumbled over the arch and together, as man and wife, they crossed the last bridge home.

* * * * *

Dear Reader,

I hope you've enjoyed Zak and Jilly's story, the final installment in the *Redemption River* series. Hanging out in this small town with Popbottle Jones, GI Jack and a cast of broken spirits who discover hope and healing has been a fulfilling experience. The books have been good to me, garnering two RITA nominations and a Booksellers' Best nomination, thanks to you, my wonderful readers. You have also written beautiful letters and emails about the way the stories have touched you and, in return, you have touched me. So, it is with bittersweet feelings that I cross the bridge to Redemption one last time and bring this series to a close.

I hope you'll look for future books by Linda Goodnight and, as always, let me know your thoughts. I can be reached through my website www.lindagoodnight.com or through my publisher, Love Inspired Books, 233 Broadway, Suite 1001, New York, NY 102790.

Until the next time, may God richly bless your life.

Linda Goodnight

Questions for Discussion

1. Which of the characters in this book was your favorite? What quality endeared him or her to you?

2. What was Zak's ambition? Do you think it was something he really wanted or only a dream? Why?

3. Jilly has a self-concept issue that holds her back from romance. What was it? Do you think her feelings were justified? Have you ever struggled with your self-concept? How did you overcome it?

4. What was Zak's motivation for taking Crystal and her children into his care? How did his feelings change during the course of the story?

5. Why did Jilly insist Zak "do the right thing" with Crystal? What was the right thing in her view? In his? How would you react to such a situation?

6. After Crystal arrives, Jilly feels guilty about her unrequited love for Zak. Is she justified in feeling this way? Or is she being self-righteous? Is love ever wrong?

7. Do you consider Zak's marriage to Crystal valid and binding according to scripture? Can there ever be a gray area in the subject of marriage?

8. What were Crystal's reasons for marrying Zak? Why did he agree? What does this tell you about Zak's character?

9. What was the theme of *The Last Bridge Home?* How does the scripture in the front of the book relate to the theme?

10. Jilly's family unintentionally damaged her belief in herself. How? Why?

11. The three children, Brandon, Jake and Bella, displayed negative behaviors when they first arrived in Redemption. What problem did each have?

12. How did Brandon's problem create conflict for Zak? What reasons did Zak give for not reporting Brandon to the authorities? Did he do the right thing?

13. The book's title, *The Last Bridge Home,* is a metaphor in at least four ways that are relevant to the story. List and discuss as many of the metaphors as you can. What did the title say to you?

14. Although Jilly told herself to stay away from Zak, she couldn't comply. Was she, as she thought, a pushover where Zak was concerned? Or was she being a good neighbor, friend and Christian? How far should a person go in helping another? Can you give a scriptural reference to support your answer?

15. Have you, like Zak, ever faced a situation where you chose to do God's will even though doing so was the more difficult course of action? What was it? And what was the outcome?

16. Alternately, has there been a time when you didn't follow God's will? What was the ultimate outcome?

INSPIRATIONAL

Wholesome romances that touch the heart and soul.

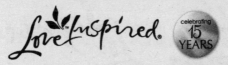

celebrating
15
YEARS

COMING NEXT MONTH
AVAILABLE FEBRUARY 28, 2012

LILAC WEDDING IN DRY CREEK
Return to Dry Creek
Janet Tronstad

DADDY LESSONS
Home to Hartley Creek
Carolyne Aarsen

TRIPLETS FIND A MOM
Annie Jones

A MAN TO TRUST
Carrie Turansky

HIGH COUNTRY HEARTS
Glynna Kaye

PICTURE PERFECT FAMILY
Renee Andrews

REQUEST YOUR FREE BOOKS!

2 FREE INSPIRATIONAL NOVELS
PLUS 2
FREE
MYSTERY GIFTS

Love Inspired

YES! Please send me 2 FREE Love Inspired® novels and my 2 FREE mystery gifts (gifts are worth about $10). After receiving them, if I don't wish to receive any more books, I can return the shipping statement marked "cancel." If I don't cancel, I will receive 6 brand-new novels every month and be billed just $4.49 per book in the U.S. or $4.99 per book in Canada. That's a saving of at least 22% off the cover price. It's quite a bargain! Shipping and handling is just 50¢ per book in the U.S. and 75¢ per book in Canada.* I understand that accepting the 2 free books and gifts places me under no obligation to buy anything. I can always return a shipment and cancel at any time. Even if I never buy another book, the two free books and gifts are mine to keep forever.

105/305 IDN FEGR

Name	(PLEASE PRINT)	
Address		Apt. #
City	State/Prov.	Zip/Postal Code

Signature (if under 18, a parent or guardian must sign)

Mail to the **Reader Service:**
IN U.S.A.: P.O. Box 1867, Buffalo, NY 14240-1867
IN CANADA: P.O. Box 609, Fort Erie, Ontario L2A 5X3

Not valid for current subscribers to Love Inspired books.

**Are you a subscriber to Love Inspired books
and want to receive the larger-print edition?
Call 1-800-873-8635 or visit www.ReaderService.com.**

* Terms and prices subject to change without notice. Prices do not include applicable taxes. Sales tax applicable in N.Y. Canadian residents will be charged applicable taxes. Offer not valid in Quebec. This offer is limited to one order per household. All orders subject to credit approval. Credit or debit balances in a customer's account(s) may be offset by any other outstanding balance owed by or to the customer. Please allow 4 to 6 weeks for delivery. Offer available while quantities last.

Your Privacy—The Reader Service is committed to protecting your privacy. Our Privacy Policy is available online at www.ReaderService.com or upon request from the Reader Service.

We make a portion of our mailing list available to reputable third parties that offer products we believe may interest you. If you prefer that we not exchange your name with third parties, or if you wish to clarify or modify your communication preferences, please visit us at www.ReaderService.com/consumerchoice or write to us at Reader Service Preference Service, P.O. Box 9062, Buffalo, NY 14269. Include your complete name and address.

LIREG11B

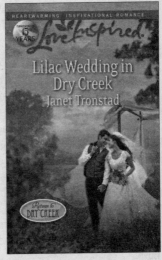

*When Cat Barker ran away from the juvenile home
she was raised in, she left her first love, Jake Stone.
Now Cat needs help, and she must turn to
her daughter's secret father.*

Read on for a sneak peek of
LILAC WEDDING IN DRY CREEK
by Janet Tronstad.

"Who's her father?" Jake's voice was low and impatient.

Cat took a quick breath. "I thought you knew. It's you."

"Me?" Jake turned to stare at her fully. She couldn't read his face. He'd gone pale. That much she could see.

She nodded and darted a look over at Lara. "I know she doesn't look like you, but I swear I wasn't with anyone else. Not after we—"

"Of course you weren't with anyone else," Jake said indignantly. "We were so tight there would have been no time to—" He lifted his hand to rub the back of his neck. "At least, I thought we were tight. Until you ran away.

"She's really mine?" he whispered, his voice husky once again.

Cat nodded. "She doesn't know. Although she doesn't take after you—her hair and everything—she's got your way of looking out at the world. I assumed someone on the staff at the youth home must have told you about her—"

His jaw tensed further at that.

"You think I wouldn't have moved heaven and earth to find you if I'd known you'd had my baby?" Jake's eyes flashed. "I tried to trace you. They said you didn't want to be found, so I finally accepted that. But if I'd known I had a daughter, I would have forced them to tell me where you were."

"But you've been sending me money. No letters. Just the money. Why would you do that? I thought it was like child support in your mind. That you wanted to be responsible even if you didn't want to be involved with us."

Jake shook his head. "I didn't know what to say. I thought the money spoke for itself. That you would write when you were ready. And I figured you could use food and things, so…"

"Charity?" she whispered, appalled. She'd never imagined that was what the envelopes of cash were about.

Jake lowered his eyes, but he didn't deny anything.

He had always been the first one to do what was right. But that didn't equal love. She knew that better than anyone, and she didn't want Lara to grow up feeling like she was a burden on someone.

Cat reminded herself that's why she had run away from Jake all those years ago. She'd known back then that he'd marry her for duty, but it wasn't enough.

Can Jake and Cat put the past behind them for the sake of their daughter?

Find out in LILAC WEDDING IN DRY CREEK by Janet Tronstad, available March 2012 from Love Inspired Books.

Love Inspired HISTORICAL

The heiress Josh O'Malley has courted by mail is on her way to Gatlinburg, Tennessee, to become his wife. But it's her sister who arrives, to end the engagement. Kate Morgan can't help but like the beautiful mountain town... and her sister's would-be groom. If only Josh would realize that his dreams of family can still come true...

The Bridal Swap
by
KAREN KIRST

SMOKY MOUNTAIN MATCHES

Available March wherever books are sold.

www.LoveInspiredBooks.com

LIH82908